S0-ARH-885

FROM THE
CREATORS OF WAGONS WEST

STAGECOACH

STATION 13:

CARSON CITY

HANK MITCHUM

THEY CAME TO CARSON CITY

Frank Gannon—A southerner who would not take sides in the Civil War, he brought his guns west and now must use them to stop the bloodshed from spilling over to the Nevada Territory.

Laura Kirby—Her skills as a nurse could not heal her own pain from the disappearance of her husband . . . and she would not rest till she found him.

Reb Jackman—The fiery raider leader would sacrifice anything—or anybody—to bring the Union to its knees.

Samuel Clemens—Lanky, young, rumpled, harddrinking, his Mark Twain flair for writing thrust him deep into the violence of Carson City.

The Stagecoach Series
Ask your bookseller for the books you have missed

STAGECOACH STATION 13:

CARSON CITY

Hank Mitchum

Created by the producers of
Wagons West, White Indian,
Saga of the Southwest, and
The Kent Family Chronicles.

Chairman of the Board: Lyle Kenyon Engel

BANTAM BOOKS
TORONTO • NEW YORK • LONDON • SYDNEY • AUCKLAND

STAGECOACH STATION 13: CARSON CITY

*A Bantam Book / published by arrangement with
Book Creations Inc.*

Bantam edition / August 1984

*Produced by Book Creations Inc.
Chairman of the Board: Lyle Kenyon Engel*

*All rights reserved.
Copyright © 1984 by Book Creations Inc.
Cover art copyright © 1984 by Guy Deel.
This book may not be reproduced in whole or in part, by
mimeograph or any other means, without permission.
For information address: Bantam Books, Inc.*

ISBN 0-553-24345-4

Published simultaneously in the United States and Canada

Bantam Books are published by Bantam Books, Inc. Its trademark, consisting of the words "Bantam Books" and the por-
trayal of a rooster, is Registered in U.S. Patent and Trademark
Office and in other countries. Marca Registrada. Bantam Books,
Inc., 666 Fifth Avenue, New York, New York 10103.

PRINTED IN THE UNITED STATES OF AMERICA

H   0 9 8 7 6 5 4 3 2 1

STAGECOACH STATION 13:

CARSON CITY

Chapter 1

Frank Gannon's dark mood matched the weather. The stagecoach he was riding east from Placerville, California, to the Washoe region of Nevada had left the springtime of May 1864 behind. Overnight, the climb into the Sierra Nevada had brought back winter. Late snowdrifts blanketed the towering granite peaks. Dropping away from Echo Summit, with Lake Tahoe to the north and Carson Valley dead ahead, the snow cover was raveling out to ragged drifts. Overhead, swollen clouds hung heavy in the sky. Sharp wind gusts raked the trees, whipped at the stagecoach, and forced Gannon and the driver, who sat beside him atop the vehicle, to pull their hat brims low and to settle deeper into their windbreakers.

The driver, a solidly built and whiskered man named Barney Powers, had taken over the reins at the last station and had been wanting to talk ever since. But he had respected Gannon's obvious desire for silence and kept his horses working in their harness as the big Concord coach rolled smoothly over the twists and turns of the mountain road. Finally, Powers blurted out the question that was eating at him. "Is it true, Frank? Are you really bein' called onto the carpet? Word's travelin' all along the line 'bout a telegram orderin' you back to Carson City. To a meetin' with old Ben Holladay!"

Gannon glanced quickly at his driver and then forward again at the horses and the road winding before them through dark ranks of timber. "I suppose bad news moves quickest," he commented dryly. "Don't

1

worry about it, Barney. It's my problem. It goes with the job."

"But it ain't fair," the driver protested angrily. "Holladay's goin' to lay it on you for everything that's gone wrong with this division. The truth is we're all of us at fault. Hell, you've been the finest boss any of us ever worked for. And here we've gone and let you down!"

"That's nonsense," Gannon said firmly, shifting his six-foot frame on the wooden seat.

"Then why are things in such a mess?"

"Not because anyone's laid down on the job," Gannon insisted. "Drivers, guards, station tenders— there's not a man in this division but would put his neck on the line for the good of the Overland. I don't need to name the ones that already have. But these past months have put us up against a situation different from any we've faced before."

"Yeah . . ." Powers said, his voice trailing away while both men thought of recent events. During the last week, another shipment of silver bullion had been stolen by outlaws, and in another incident, two company men had been killed at Eagle Point Station and all the stage-line horses stolen from the corral.

"The fact remains," Gannon went on, "Holladay promoted me and put me in charge of this final stretch west of Carson City. He's going to want to know why things haven't been ironed out. It's his right—and he can't be blamed for not being interested in excuses."

Silence once again fell between the two men. As the morning wore on the road gradually dropped out of the higher reaches of the hills. Low clouds continued to scuttle before the push of crosscurrents, but the coach was protected by the mountains. Frank Gannon knew every mile of the Kingsbury grade, every pass and switchback. Before his promotion to division agent, he had driven plenty of stages over it himself. Only a few years earlier, this heavily traveled route between California and the Comstock region of Nevada had been a tortuous thoroughfare of wheel ruts worn into barren rock. Thousands of travelers had crossed it, along with tons of freighted supplies for Nevada's burgeoning silver camps and millions of dollars in Washoe silver. The toll road had been macadamized for its entire length at a reputed cost of more than fifty thousand dollars. The paving job had smoothed out some of the most arduous places and shaved a little off the twenty-four-hour run for Ben Holladay's Overland Mail and Express Company stage line.

Still, the trip could be a tough haul for both vehicles and team horses, to say nothing of the passengers, who had to endure to exhaustion the constant sway and jostling as they sat on the crowded coach seats or clung to places on the roof, with only the briefest of stops at the scattered stage stations.

The coach on which Frank Gannon rode had left Placerville the previous evening at dusk. It had been a bone-chilling night and a bleak and sunless morning, but without any real incident. Gannon had had plenty of time during the trip to think about the telegram in his pocket and about the meeting that awaited him with his employer. As noon approached, the stagecoach came through a shallow pass, and suddenly Carson Valley opened before it under weak shafts of sunlight spearing through broken fields of clouds. The toll road leveled off. Just where it joined the ancient emigrant route, a cluster of buildings marked one of the Overland's principal stations.

It was a peaceful scene. Smoke rose from the chimney of the main house, and a couple of stock tenders stood ready to unhook the tired stage horses and replace them with fresh teams. Barney Powers yelled to spur his horses into a faster pace, bringing his coach in with grand style. As they rolled nearer he looked at Gannon and said, "Well—so far, so good. We're out of the hills, practically into civilization. Ain't likely now we'd run into trouble."

"We'll hope so." Gannon was not inclined to take anything for granted.

The station came alive as they rolled in. Stock tenders waved and yelled a greeting, and the station-master came out onto the porch to watch them arrive. Powers brought his horses up with a flourish that set the big Concord coach rocking on its thoroughbraces; then he stayed aboard while the lathered horses were being unhitched. Frank Gannon stepped down from the high front wheel and swung the iron step into position. He opened the door of the coach for his weary and half-frozen passengers, who climbed stiffly but gratefully from their places.

Of the eight people in the stage, all but one were men. They were the usual mixed bag, including a couple whom Gannon knew personally—a mine superintendent from the Comstock and a law clerk returning to his post at the Nevada territorial capital in Carson City.

It was the woman who had caught Gannon's attention. It was only natural that she would, since she was alone in a coach full of male strangers. Throughout the dark night Gannon had wondered how she was, wrapped in the robes and blankets the stage line provided and with men sleeping or talking around her. The fact that she was uncommonly pretty—blue-eyed under a wing of auburn hair that showed beneath the edge of the hat she wore for traveling—had made him take particular notice of her the moment he first saw her waiting to board the stage at Placerville.

He took her hand to help her down and was surprised by her strong, sure grip. Her step was light in spite of the cramp and chill of hours on a crowded coach seat. "You can see we're down off the mountains," he told her. "The rest of the way will be level going. I hope you haven't had too bad a time of it."

The answering look she gave him was direct, making him suddenly conscious of his two-days' stubble of beard. There was a distinct reserve in her voice as she said, "I'm fine, thank you. Famished, at the moment."

Gannon nodded toward the station. "Here's the place to take care of that. A good, hot meal will be welcome for all of us."

"I've never made this trip," she remarked. "How much longer is it to Carson City?"

"There'll be one more stop, at Genoa. We should hit Carson City well before dark." She thanked him with a smile and a nod. It was the thought of her alone in a strange place that bothered Gannon enough to venture a personal question. "Will you be meeting someone?"

He had thought it would be harmless enough to ask, but perhaps it had been a mistake. As though resenting his curiosity, she withdrew behind rather cool formality and her answer was brief. "Yes, I am. My husband."

"I see."

As he stood aside so she could move toward the station building, he had a rueful sensation of having been put in his place.

A voice from inside the coach commented, "That's a handsome young lady. Married, unfortunately."

The last person to step down from the coach was a tall, spare, and grizzled man in a canvas windbreaker, slightly stooped but with a hint of strength in the set of his jaw and with intelligence in the eyes that peered from beneath a gray thicket of brow.

Gannon nodded. "She just now told me she'd be meeting her husband at Carson City."

"Then you got as much out of her as I've managed in all the time since we left Placerville. I guess she's pretty enough to be choosy about who she talks to and how much she says. I did get her name, at least. It's Kirby—Laura Kirby, I believe she said. I never learned anything at all about her husband."

Since Gannon considered this to be no business of either of them, he thought it time to change the subject. "I don't remember that we introduced ourselves. I'm Frank Gannon," he said.

The other man nodded. "I already know who you are—division agent for the Overland. My name's Fox. Linus Fox," he said, offering his strong but bony hand.

Gannon indicated the front of the other man's coat. "Did I see a sheriff's star under there?"

Linus Fox pulled aside the front of the canvas jacket, revealing the metal star pinned to the front of the coat he wore underneath. "I carry the badge over at San Andreas," he explained, "north of Placerville. I guess by rights I really should take it off while I'm outside my own bailiwick—the gun, too." He touched the revolver in its well-worn holster, which he carried openly on his right leg.

"Fact is," Sheriff Fox went on, "I'm here on business. Got extradition papers on a prisoner in the pen at Carson City. Soon as I have your Nevada governor's John Hancock, I can collect my man and take him back to California to hang for murder. I was wanting to ask you if there'll be any problem taking him on the stage."

"Not so long as you keep him under control," Gannon replied.

"Don't worry. I intend to handle this fellow with real caution. I understand he's something of a wild man when he's crossed. A couple years ago, before my time, he tried to hold up a store and went berserk. Put three bullets into the owner when the man argued with him. He was tried and convicted but killed a guard and got away 'fore they could hang him. Nothing more was seen or heard of him after that, until a story in a newspaper said he'd been arrested and convicted here in Nevada—for stage robbery."

Gannon looked up sharply. "Stage robbery? What's the man's name?"

"Bart Kramer. You know about him?" Fox asked, curious about Gannon's reaction to the name.

"I should. I helped put him in prison. There's been a gang operating in these mountains. They've given us nothing but trouble on this stretch of the

Overland, west of Carson City. With a hundred miles of toll road to cover, there's nothing much the stage line, or the local law, has been able to do." Gannon shook his head ruefully.

"Just once," he went on, "we've laid hands on a member of the gang. During a raid on one of our treasure coaches, we were able to drive them off—and this Kramer had his horse shot out from under him. We nabbed him before he could get away. The sheriff tried everything he could think of to get some information out of him—who the gang was, where they operated out of, anything. The fellow was too tough, couldn't be made to open his mouth." Gannon kicked at a rock in the road and brushed a shock of brown hair from his forehead.

"Finally there was nothing to do but try him on the evidence. We had only the one count against him. I testified at the trial. He was convicted, and the judge gave him a full twenty years, but made it clear there could probably be a shorter sentence if Kramer would only decide to open up and inform on the rest of his gang."

"But no luck?" Sheriff Fox asked.

"It's been over a month and he hasn't opened his mouth—either from sheer stubbornness or his own strange notions of honor. Given enough time, we'd thought he might still soften up and decide to talk." With a sharp look at the lawman from California, he added, "But now you show up, wanting to take him out of our hands and *hang* him—close his mouth forever."

A sudden coldness settled between the two men. The lawman considered Gannon for a moment, then said, "Yes, I can see you might object to that. I'm sorry. But according to the law, murder has to take precedence over other crimes. Soon as these extradition papers are signed I'll be taking Bart Kramer back to California. If possible, I'd like to do my job without raising any hard feelings. But I intend to do it!"

They stared at each other. "I suppose you're only doing your job," Gannon said flatly.

"I hope we can manage to be civil about it, at least." From an inner pocket Sheriff Fox produced a leather cigar case, opened it, and offered it to the other man. Gannon hesitated, then accepted one of the cigars with a nod.

"Thanks," he said. "I'll save it for after dinner." They followed the rest of the passengers into the station.

When Gannon lit up his cigar an hour later, the stagecoach was rolling once again, behind fresh and rested teams. He got the cigar burning smoothly, and the wind of their passage carried the smoke across his shoulder. He found himself thinking of Laura Kirby, recalling the hesitant smile she had given him as he helped her back into the coach. Perhaps she had wanted to make amends for her earlier brusqueness, he thought. At least he chose to take it that way. A Virginian by birth, Frank Gannon still retained a Southerner's idealistic attitude toward women, in spite of the time he had spent on the frontier. He tended to think of them as something apart and very special. And though Laura Kirby traveled alone in a rough country, and with great self-reliance, there was something—perhaps in her very directness—he found attractive about her.

But with Carson City only hours away, Gannon told himself he had better start thinking about his approaching meeting with Ben Holladay.

Word of his employer's coming had been wired from Salt Lake City to Placerville. Though no purpose for the summons had been mentioned, Gannon had no doubt why he was being called back. He already had decided there was nothing to do but to be completely open and frank about the problems besetting his stretch of the Overland on the border between Nevada and California. After all, Holladay, back in his eastern office, had an uncanny way of seeming to know everything anyhow. Gannon was grateful for his promotion. He had done his best, and it was for Holladay to decide whether he should continue in the job.

The new teams of horses had settled to a familiar, mile-eating gait. The road was level, running north along the old Emigrant Road with the sage flats of Carson Valley wheeling past on the right and sparsely timbered foothills lifting dramatically above them on the left. As Gannon gazed at the scenery, a wink of reflected sunlight caught the corner of his eye.

Instantly alert, he peered closely in the direction of the flash but saw nothing except rocks and trees. But he knew that momentary flash could only have been reflected from metal. Instinctively Gannon leaned forward, groping for the rifle underneath the seat. Even as his hands closed on the weapon he heard the unmistakable report of a gunshot. Its echoes were still bouncing along the hills as he straightened with the rifle in his hands, looking for a target.

He glimpsed a faint wisp of powder smoke, but it was instantly lost in the screen of scrub timber and the forward motion of the coach. A sound from the driver next to him made Gannon turn in alarm. Barney Powers was beginning to slide off the seat into the boot, his head hanging loosely to one side, the reins slipping from his grasp. Gannon caught a glimpse of blood but knew there was no time to learn where or how badly Powers was hurt. He let go of his rifle and grabbed for the leather reins, barely managing to trap them before they were lost.

Making sure the stagecoach did not race out of control must be his only concern. All he could do for Barney Powers was to ram an elbow against the man and try to keep his limp body from sliding farther off the seat. Genoa lay ahead. There the wounded man could be tended to. At the moment Gannon had to get the stage and its passengers to safety.

He heard more shooting—hand guns, this time— and glimpsed a line of horsemen racing down a gully toward the road. From one of the coach windows below him, a gun suddenly opened up. Gannon yelled at the startled horses, shaking the lines to straighten them out. Instantly the horses lunged into their harness, and the stage gave a lurch as it picked up speed, leaving the attackers behind.

One persistent thought forced its way into Frank's mind as he drove the team for all it was worth: If he had not caught that wink of sunlight on a rifle barrel and hastily reached into the boot for his own weapon, he would probably have taken the bullet that had passed above his bent shoulders and struck Barney Powers instead.

The unknown enemies of the Overland Stage might have discovered that the division agent was riding this particular coach into Carson City. Gannon shuddered involuntarily at his next thought: That bullet could actually have been meant for him!

Chapter 2

Genoa, originally called Mormon Station, had been the earliest settlement in what would become the Territory of Nevada. When it was founded in 1851, the Saints, as the Mormons were known, still considered the area part of their State of Deseret. But the Saints had pulled out during the so-called Mormon War with the United States in 1857, and the town had supposedly received its new name because the abrupt rise of hills behind it reminded someone of the northern coast of Italy. Its score of frame and brick buildings, huddled close against the massive granite foothills, boasted perhaps two hundred inhabitants in all. Not unnaturally, Genoa had expected to become the capital of the new territory, but it lost out to the upstart neighboring community of Carson City, some thirteen miles north.

The sudden appearance of the stage, tearing in behind lathered horses, was enough to send shock waves rippling through the settlement and to bring half its people pouring out into the crooked street. Frank Gannon drove the stage up to the galleried front of the Raycraft Hotel, suddenly tromping on the brake, which set the big red coach rocking on its thoroughbraces and caused the excited horses to mill and narrowly avoid tangling their harness. "Hurry! Fetch the doctor," he shouted to the first man he saw. "I've got a badly hurt man here."

"Not too bad hurt, I hope." Joe Raycraft, a solidly built man with a drooping mustache, spade beard, and thinning hair, had stepped out onto the porch of his hotel. "Gannon, I'm afraid Doc rode out somewhere

11

this morning on business. I don't reckon he's back
yet."

The news made Gannon swear.

"What happened?" Raycraft asked.

"We ran into an ambush. I don't know how bad
Barney Powers was hit, but he's bleeding and was
knocked out by the shock. Somebody give me a hand
here," he called down to the crowd that had quickly
gathered around the stagecoach.

At once, bystanders hurried forward to receive the
wounded man's weight as Gannon eased Powers into
their waiting hands.

"How about DeLong—the barber?" one man suggested. "He pulled a tooth for me once."

That drew a snort of disdain from a second man. "If
DeLong ever saw this much blood, he'd likely drop
over in a faint!"

"Well, we've got to do something," Joe Raycraft
said quickly. "Bring him in the hotel. I'll show you
where to put him."

The wounded driver was carried around the coach
and up the steps of the hotel, his head lolling from side
to side and his jacket open to reveal the blood soaking
the left side of his shirt. Gannon spotted a hostler from
Tingham's Livery, where the Overland boarded its extra teams. He motioned the man over and indicated the
lathered horses, "Run these animals to the barn and see
to them, but hold up with fresh teams until I give the
word. Is Chuck Drury in town?"

"I think so," the man replied.

"Then before you do anything else, you'd better
locate him and let him know he'll be taking this run the
rest of the way into Carson City."

The hostler hurried off, and Gannon swung down
from his place. The coach passengers were already getting out, obviously shaken by the ambush and by their
wild dash into town. Bystanders crowded around asking
questions. Gannon impatiently shoved his way through,
concerned for Barney Powers. He began to hurry up

the hotel steps, but a hand touched his elbow and Laura Kirby's voice halted him. "Please! I'd like to help," she told him quickly.

He was touched by her offer. "That's very kind," he said, "but I really don't think there's anything for you to do, Mrs. Kirby. Without a doctor, we can only try to make him as comfortable as possible."

"You don't understand. I know something about bullet wounds," she said.

Gannon's brown eyes stared. "You do?"

Laura frowned at his tone. "You don't believe me? I've worked with my father—a very good doctor in Sacramento. I just might be able to do something for your friend. If you'll let me, I'd be happy to try."

"Well—of course," Gannon said quickly. He was still dubious, but she was obviously sincere. "I wasn't questioning your word. I'm just surprised. Come along, then. Let's find out where they've taken him."

Barney Powers had been laid on the bed in a ground-floor room. He looked bad. His features were colorless with shock, and his skin was cold. He lay on his back, unconscious, and he didn't move when Gannon ripped open the blood-soaked shirt. A glance told the story. The bullet, coming from behind at a downward angle, had struck below the arm on Powers's left side and had torn an ugly, slanting furrow.

The three people beside the bed looked at the wound in silence that was broken only by the hurt man's quick and labored breathing. "The bleeding seems to have stopped," Gannon said.

"It could be a great deal worse," Laura Kirby observed. "You can see the bullet passed through." Gannon looked at her. She was pale but quite calm and very sure of herself as she continued. "It would help if we could have a lamp here, for better light. And perhaps if someone could find a knife—something with a sharp point that I can use as a probe. There may be splinters of bone from a rib, or even a bit of shattered lead. They could still damage his lung if they aren't removed."

Something in the matter-of-fact way she talked about the problem made Gannon's remaining doubts about her disappear. He glanced at Raycraft and found the hotel owner staring at the young woman. Gannon explained, "Mrs. Kirby's had medical training, and she's offered her services. Can you get her what she needs?"

The hotelman found his voice. "Why, sure. Sure thing!"

"Hot water, too, of course," Laura Kirby added as he turned away. "And if you will, something I can use for bandages."

As the sun outside went behind a cloud, the room darkened. Gannon found an oil lamp and a block of sulfur matches on the commode. He lit the lamp and brought it over to the small bedside table. Laura was examining the wound when Joe Raycraft returned carrying a steaming pitcher of hot water. He had a dish towel over one arm and a narrow-bladed carving knife. Laura nodded her approval.

Her first act was to pour some of the water into a china washbowl, and after rolling up the sleeves of her blouse, she scrubbed her hands with a bar of strong yellow soap. Joe Raycraft watched her with a quizzical expression, finally blurting out, "Ma'am, ain't you doing things a little backwards? Seems like afterwards is when you'll need a good washing up!"

Laura looked at him. "Maybe it's because I'm a woman, Mr. Raycraft," she said. "A lot of doctors don't bother about such matters—but one thing I know, I would never dream of fixing a meal without washing my hands first. I can't see that this is any different." She proceeded to clean the blade of the knife, testing its sharp point on her finger. Then she approached the unconscious man on the bed.

Again Gannon saw the pallor and tension in her face. "You're sure you wouldn't like one of us to do this?" he suggested.

"Have you done it before, Mr. Gannon?"

"No," he admitted.

"I have." She smiled briefly. "I'd appreciate it though, if you two men would hold him. I doubt that he's going to feel anything, but it would be bad if he happened to make any sudden movements."

Gannon and Raycraft placed themselves where they could put a firm grip on Barney Powers as the young woman took a quick breath and settled to her work. Only a faint fluttering at the corners of her eyes showed the strain she was under. Her knife hand appeared steady. She worked by feel, almost as though the gently probing point of the knife was an extension of her fingers. She discovered a shred of material from Powers's jacket that the bullet had carried with it, and she deftly plucked the material free.

Gannon found himself forgetting to breathe. Once, Barney Powers gave a faint moan and tried to stir. Gannon quickly clamped down on the unconscious man's shoulder and arm to hold him steady. At the first hint of movement Laura Kirby had snatched the knife away. When Gannon felt Powers's muscles relax, he nodded that it was safe for her to continue.

Word of what was happening in the hotel room seemed to have spread through the town. Gannon began to be aware of whispers and jostling in the hallway beyond the open door. Someone said in an awed voice, half aloud but quite distinctly, "Look at that, would you—a *lady doctor!* Whatever the hell next, d'you suppose?" Gannon looked up sharply and gave the onlookers a stare and a shake of the head that silenced them.

At last Laura straightened, gave a long sigh, and put the knife aside. She was pleased her efforts had not started the wound bleeding again, and she said, "That should do. The wound is clean, in good shape to mend. Do you have any alcohol?" she asked Raycraft.

"That's one thing we got plenty of," the hotelman said, and went to get it. He was back almost at once with a half-filled bottle of whiskey. As the young woman applied it to the raw wound, the bite of it caused

Powers to jerk and cry out. But he slumped back again, and Laura swiftly proceeded to dress the wound with a compress and bandages torn from the material she had been given.

The hurt man's breathing deepened and steadied. "He's sleeping now," Laura told them. "I think I'd better let it go at this. Your doctor may decide to take some stitches. For the present, the injured man should just be kept quiet."

"I'll see to that," Raycraft assured her. "Somehow I got a feeling he won't want to do anything else for a while!"

As they looked at the man sleeping on the bed, Frank Gannon told her earnestly, "I can't thank you enough. You did a good job. I can understand that fellow's surprise, just now, at the sight of a lady doctor. I know *I* never met one before."

Fastening a cuff of her blouse, Laura fixed her blue eyes on him. "You still haven't. Oh, someday I hope women will be encouraged to enroll in medical school and study for a license. But so far only a handful have been accepted."

Gannon wasn't surprised. Of all the professions that remained closed to women, surely medicine would be one of the last male bastions to fall. He said, "Anyhow, I must say your pa taught you well."

She gave him a brief smile. "Thank you."

"And I think I can tell you this much. If there's any reason you might be looking for work in Carson City, after what I've just seen I can introduce you to at least one doctor who'd be glad to hire you on a moment's notice."

"Oh?" She seemed to consider what he had told her for a moment. "Thank you. I might want to remember that."

On the hotel veranda, Sheriff Fox stood smoking one of his ever-present cigars as he leaned both hands on the railing and looked at the sky of broken clouds. The afternoon sunlight drew tendrils of steam from the muddy street where the stagecoach stood idle. As Gannon approached him, the sheriff straightened and looked expectantly past him. "Where's the lady doctor?" he asked.

"Mrs. Kirby? She wanted to stay and keep an eye on Barney until it's time to leave."

"She beats all, don't she?" the grizzled lawman muttered. "It's the only thing anybody here seems able to talk about. What do *you* think, Gannon? Could you really stand to have a woman doctor working on you?"

Frank Gannon hesitated. "The idea might take some getting used to," he admitted. "Maybe the time will come. I do know I'd rather be in the hands of someone like Mrs. Kirby than some of the drunks and butchers I've run into since I came west."

Fox still appeared dubious, but he let the question drop. "How's your driver making out?"

"She thinks he's going to be all right—though it will take a little time before he's able to sit on the box and handle the reins again."

Linus Fox blew a smoke ring and watched it dissolve against the ceiling of the veranda. "You know," he said suddenly, "I been giving some thought to that shooting. Where you were sitting, next to the driver, you'd have been between him and the rifle. Is there a chance the bullet might've had *your* name on it, instead of his?"

Gannon gave him a sharp look. "So you thought of that, too? As a matter of fact, I had caught the reflection of sunlight on the barrel and was leaning down to get my own rifle when the shot came. In order to hit Barney Powers at the angle it did, the slug couldn't have missed me by more than inches."

"That must give you a funny feeling," the lawman said dryly. "Would you guess it was something personal? I mean, d'you suppose they knew it was *you* sitting there—a key man with the Overland, not some hired shotgun messenger?"

"I think it's only smart to figure so," Gannon said regretfully.

"You could be right. When those horsemen got closer, I managed to throw off a few shots myself. Of course I only had my six-shooter," the sheriff added, laying a hand on it. "And we were all getting thrown around in there, the way you were making those horses scoot. But I think I nailed one of the bastards."

"Oh? You did?" Gannon drew himself to his full height in surprise.

"Yeah, I'm pretty sure. It looked like I nearly knocked him out of the saddle. That was all I had time to see, before we'd left them behind. Everything happened so fast, it occurs to me they might still be under the impression you were the one who collected that rifle bullet."

Gannon considered the idea, but he shook his head. "If they are, I imagine it won't take them long to learn their mistake—whoever they are."

A young man with a sunburnt face came across the muddy street to the foot of the hotel steps. "Gannon?" he called up. "I heard you were wantin' me?"

"That's right, Chuck," Gannon told him. "I need you to take over the reins for Barney Powers and run this stage into Carson City. I want to be pulling out as soon as new teams are in place."

"Yes, sir. I'll see to it right away." Chuck Drury hurried off in the direction of the livery stable.

The crowd that had gathered to watch the arrival of the stage had scattered after the excitement was over. The sun was dropping toward the rampart of foothills that rose behind the town, and a chill wind had sprung up. "Guess I'd better go look for my passengers," Gannon said.

"I saw most of them drifting over toward that saloon in the next block," Linus Fox told him. "You should find them there."

"Thanks."

Livingston's Exchange was a squat brick building

beyond a cross street and a few yards north of the hotel. An L-shaped wooden bar took up half the low-ceilinged room, the remaining space being occupied by a few tables and stools. Quite a few of the crowd that had been in the street earlier appeared to have drifted into the bar. Gannon spotted his missing passengers fortifying themselves for the last part of their journey. He stopped in the doorway a moment, waiting for the chance to make an announcement.

A big, yellow-haired, heavily bearded man stood at the bar clutching a beer mug in one huge hand. He had the look of one of the teamsters who hauled supplies for the Comstock region across the toll road from California, and he was holding forth in a booming voice on the latest war news.

With Grant and Lee locked in a bloody stalemate in the wilderness, the three-year-old war between the states was causing a heightening of partisan feeling even in a place as far removed from the fighting as a Nevada bar. The big teamster was pro-Union, and he was holding back nothing of his hatred for those he called slavers, secessionists, and copperheads. Gannon thought the teamster was deliberately goading his audience, trying to start an argument, but they listened in silence as though not inclined to oblige anyone who was set on trouble.

Then Gannon noticed one of the stage passengers standing alone where the angle of the bar front joined the side wall. It was Tim Johnson, a thin-faced young man, probably not even twenty, with a wild shock of black hair and an unassertive but determined manner. In a voice that held the drawl of the deep South he had explained to Gannon that having come to California some years ago with a pair of older cousins, he was leaving them and returning home. Though Johnson did not say it was in order to enlist in the Confederate Army, Gannon had no doubt that was the young man's purpose.

Like the rest in the room, Johnson had been listening in silence to the harangue. But as the big fellow paused for a drag at the beer he was holding, young Johnson spoke up in a mild tone. "Bartender? How about settin' 'em up all around? Let's make it one for old South Carolina—and the great Confed'racy!"

Everyone in the room froze. The man behind the bar made no move, taking the order as being a rhetorical flourish. The flourish had not failed to make its point. The teamster stiffened with his beer mug half raised. He set it down and deliberately shouldered past his neighbors to stride around the angle of the bar.

The challenger stood and watched him come. The teamster topped Johnson by nearly a head, and the young man's face drained of color, but his manner was unyielding. Gannon grimaced, wondering if Tim Johnson really thought he could handle what he had started.

"Hell!" the big man said loudly. "I ain't drinkin' with no dirty Secesh! From Carolina, you said?"

"That's right," the young fellow answered in a quiet voice, which nevertheless managed to be heard throughout the room. "I'm on my way back there now to get in on the fight. Help set the Yankees packin' and headin' no'th where they belong."

"You think so? Looks like I just better stomp on you, here and now—save somebody the trouble of doin' it later!" The big man reached for the youngster.

But Johnson was wiry and quick. He lashed a punch into the bearded face that obviously carried a sting. It held the teamster up for a moment and made him shake his head in surprise. But only for a moment. Then he shot out a hand that grabbed the young man's shoulder before the smaller man could dodge away. Gannon saw Johnson wince under the pressure. Holding Johnson firmly, the big man brought his other fist around and slammed it into the side of the youngster's head. The sound of the blow was distinctly audible. Tim Johnson crumpled, and the teamster let him go, landing limply at the foot of the bar.

The people in the bar were all on their feet, yelling

as they craned and jostled to see what would happen next. On a sudden hunch, Gannon propelled himself forward. The teamster had kicked a bar stool out of his way and was slowly circling the prone figure. He lifted one heavy cowhide boot, clearly intent on doing just what he had promised to do by stomping his opponent into the floor. But Gannon got there before the boot could land. He caught the big man by a shoulder and jerked him around. "You've already hurt him. Let it go!" he said sharply.

His interference only earned him a yell of rage from the teamster. One of the man's huge fists reached for him. Gannon had little trouble dodging it, nor did he waste his strength punching at the other man's rock-solid jaw. Gannon had already noticed that for all his opponent's hard muscle, a liking for beer had created a soft bulge in the region of the teamster's belt buckle. Gannon aimed for the bulge and felt his fist sink deep. The man was driven backward and doubled over. His face turned purple. Men scrambled out of his way as the teamster sat down abruptly with his back against the bar.

One look at the big man's gaping mouth and bulging eyes told Gannon this was a man who blustered and then crumpled once he found himself hurt. Gannon promptly dismissed him. Young Johnson was already struggling to his feet, and Gannon hooked an arm under him and helped him up. Looking about, the Overland agent picked out his passengers from among the silently staring crowd and announced, "The stage will be rolling in about five minutes. Be on it if you don't want to get left." With that he turned Tim Johnson toward the door and steered him outside.

They slowly walked to the front of the hotel, where fresh teams had been brought from the livery and were being hooked into the harness. Gannon eased the boy down onto a crude wooden bench and gave him a handkerchief to wipe the blood from his cheek where the teamster's heavy knuckles had broken the skin. Still shaken, the young fellow muttered, "That peckerwood had him a fist that would drop a mule!"

"He's a muleskinner—it goes with the job," Gannon pointed out. "Next time, just be more careful who you pick a fight with."

"Hell, I couldn't stand any more of his talk!"

"How old are you?" Gannon asked suddenly.

The youngster bristled. "I'm old enough to do my job!"

"Yes." Gannon nodded, his expression bleak. "I don't doubt but what you are," he said sourly. "The rate the Confederacy is using itself up, it'll be putting even younger lads than you in the field. The South simply hasn't got the manpower the North has."

"And what are *you* doin' about it?" Suddenly Tim Johnson was on his feet, facing Gannon. "Mister, you ain't no Yankee! Reckon I should know the South when I hear it talkin'. To me you sound like a Virginian."

Gannon smile kindly. "You have a good ear."

"I also know you ain't skeered, not the way you walked up to that bruiser in there! I'm grateful to you for it, sir. But why is it you ain't back home helpin' out, now that the South has its back to the wall?"

His words stung Gannon more than he liked to admit. It made his voice cold. "If you have to know, it's because I'm convinced our side is wrong. Not only about slavery—though I was dead set against putting my life on the line for the benefit of the plantation owners. But there's more to it than that. I just can't get around what Mr. Lincoln says about not busting up our country. There'll always be something around for men to quarrel over. Let the South go because of slavery, and pretty soon it'll be something else—and after that, something else again. The Confederacy will fly apart the same way. It looks to me there'll be no place to stop until the whole country's broken down into separate little states, all squabbling among themselves."

"I don't believe that!" Tim Johnson said stoutly.

"You'd better believe it! And while you're at it, ask

yourself what all those kings in Europe are going to be doing in the meantime. There's nothing they'd like better than the chance to come over and pick us off one by one. That would put an end, for good, to what we were after when we got rid of King George—and tried to prove that ordinary men really can govern themselves." Gannon's deep brown eyes were fixed intently on the young man.

"Let 'em try!" Johnson exclaimed. "They do, and we'll give 'em what we gave the British!"

Gannon shrugged, realizing the young man was too worked up to listen to rational arguments. "All right. You go on believing that, son—if you can. But I think the South has made a damned sad mistake. On the other hand, when it came right down to it, there was no way I could take up a gun against my neighbors and friends. I found myself torn two ways. And since I couldn't fight on either side, I did the only thing I could. I got out. I came west in sixty-one, and now I really can't see myself ever going back east again."

From the boy's black and stubborn scowl, Gannon knew his arguments had fallen on deaf ears. He sighed. "There's no point in the two of us fighting. Everybody else seems ready to climb back on the stage. What do you say we go join them?"

Chapter 3

From the day the promoters of Carson City had laid it out in 1858, they had meant big things for the town. Even in the beginning they had been sure someday it would be the seat of government for a new state. Accordingly they had left an open square where the future capitol would stand. Having named their town for Kit Carson—the scout and Indian fighter who had once led the explorer General John Charles Fremont through the area—they sat back to await the future.

Developments came fast. Within a year, the big strike on the Comstock Lode had turned out to be the richest body of silver ore ever uncovered. And when the war between North and South began, Washington found that it desperately needed that wealth. Soon Nevada Territory was organized. In the spring of 1864, the enabling act had been passed that would make Nevada the thirty-sixth state as soon as its citizens could quit squabbling over a constitution. The territorial supreme court and assembly continued to meet in rented rooms scattered about the town. But government buildings and even a mint for the coining of Comstock silver were on the drawing boards. On the coattails of Virginia City, Carson City was booming, too.

Spring was trying to get a toehold in Carson Valley, but fresh snow streaked the Sierra foothills that rose immediately behind the town. As dusk began to fall, Chuck Drury, the replacement driver, whipped up his teams to a gallop and guided them into Carson Street. The stagecoach pulled to an abrupt halt before a squat

24

stone building that housed the station and local office of the farflung Overland stage line.

As Gannon swung down from the top of the coach, his chief clerk, Wade Holbrook, came out to greet him and to catch the mail sack Drury tossed down. "Is Ben Holladay in town?" Gannon asked.

"Not yet, but he's expected," Holbrook reported. "We got another wire, saying to look for him this evening."

"All right. When he shows, tell him I'll be checking back." Gannon turned to open the door of the stagecoach and to drop the iron step into place. "This is Carson City," he informed the passengers. "Those who are going on will have an hour to get something to eat. You'll find there are several pretty good places along the street, here. Try to be back on time so we don't have to go looking for you."

He helped Laura Kirby down the long step to the ground and received a brief nod of thanks. Wade Holbrook had unfastened the leather shield covering the coach's rear boot, and Mrs. Kirby joined the other passengers who were waiting to claim their luggage. Young Tim Johnson stepped out, and the eyes in his bruised face met Gannon's uncertainly before he turned away without speaking. Remembering their discussion in Genoa, Gannon suddenly took a step after the boy.

"Johnson . . ." The young man turned, still scowling. "We won't be meeting again," Gannon said in a friendly tone. "I hope you didn't take offense at anything I may have said. The two of us don't happen to agree on what we should do about the war. But each of us is doing what he thinks he has to do. I just want to wish you the best of luck where you're going."

Tim Johnson looked at the hand Gannon extended. "All right," he said, taking it. "Thanks. I guess luck is somethin' I'm gonna need!"

"No hard feelings?" Gannon's faced crinkled in a smile.

"After what you done for me in that saloon?" the

younger man asked gruffly, shaking hands firmly. Then he quickly walked toward an eating place whose windows were glowing invitingly in the waning day. Gannon knew he was seeing Tim Johnson for the last time. Thinking of all the young men on both sides who were being sacrificed in the seemingly unending war suddenly made Gannon very sad.

Laura Kirby stood by the rear of the stagecoach with an awkward-looking carpetbag at her feet, glancing around uncertainly at the unfamiliar town. Gannon hesitated to intrude, but she appeared vulnerable and even a little frightened, her wrap drawn against the chill of the night wind coming off the hills behind the town. He went over to her.

"You don't see your husband yet, Mrs. Kirby? You're welcome to wait inside the station for him," he said, gesturing behind him.

She looked up, startled. "Oh . . . thank you very much, but I guess . . ." Under Gannon's steady gaze she seemed to falter for a moment, then continued. "To tell you the truth, Jim may not really have known—not for sure—that I'd be arriving today," she admitted.

Gannon smiled reassuringly. "I see. Well, you can leave word for him at the station and I don't think you'll have any trouble finding a place to stay until he comes looking for you. There are hotels, rooming houses. . . ."

"Yes, I'm sure I'll be quite all right," she broke in, then hesitated again. "There *is* one thing." She drew breath. "Mr. Gannon, I've been thinking over what you said about my being able to find employment here in Carson City."

"There's not the least doubt of it," Gannon said firmly. "For one thing, I know my friend Doc Howard would be more than glad to snap up a trained assistant. I'd be glad to have a word with him."

"Thank you. I'd appreciate it," the young woman said gratefully.

"Better yet, his office is only a couple of blocks

away from here. We could drop around there right now, and see if he's in," Gannon suggested.

Mrs. Kirby hesitated. "Only if you're sure I'm not being too much bother."

"No bother at all. Come along." Gannon picked up her bag and pointed the way.

Dr. Howard had his office in a small, neat clapboard building that was painted white but lacked any kind of trim. An iron hitching post stood in front of the building for his customers to tie their animals. The windows were dark, and a card in the window of the closed door read, *Gone to supper*. There also was an address on Division Street printed in smaller letters.

"That's the widow Devere's place," Gannon explained. "She often has the doc over for meals, and nobody could blame him for going. He lives alone, and there's not a better cook in town than Madge Devere. We'll try there."

Mrs. Kirby caught his arm. "Oh, no! That would be intruding."

"I don't think so. With George Howard you have to be ready to catch him when you have the chance. Besides," he went on, guiding her along the darkening street, "it would be nice for you to know Madge, even if you don't plan to be in town long. She's a fine woman, a good person to have for a friend. She came here with her husband, an attorney—a man who promised to have a fine career with the state government once it got set up. But Tom Devere came down with pneumonia, and in spite of everything Doc tried he wasn't able to pull Tom through. In a matter of weeks Tom was gone, just like that—in the prime of life."

"How very sad!" Laura exclaimed.

"It sure was," Gannon agreed. "He left Madge with the house he'd built for her, but hardly any money. But she kept going. What is it they call someone who makes hats for ladies?" He looked at Laura with a quizzical frown.

"A milliner?"

"That's right. Anyway, that's what Madge does. She turned her parlor into a workroom and she's mighty good at it. Of course, I don't know much about such things, but she takes her hats up to Virginia City and sells them to the stores where the mineowners' wives do their trading. And they always seem to want more. Anyway, she's quite a person. I have an idea you'll like her."

The Devere house on Division Street was not at all elaborate, simply a two-story frame structure with a side porch, a tall brick chimney, and scrollwork along the gables. But it had an air of solid hominess, with plants lining the brick walk that led from the gate in the picket fence to the front door. Gannon turned the knob of the doorbell, and through the glass they saw a woman approaching from the door at the far end of the center hall.

She opened the door and smiled broadly as she recognized Gannon. "Oh, it's you, Frank. Come in."

"Is Doc here?" he asked.

"He is indeed. We were just about to sit down to dinner. Come on back to the kitchen."

As they stepped into the hall Gannon introduced his companion. "Mrs. Kirby would like to see Doc for a minute, if it's not inconvenient."

"Nothing seriously wrong, I hope?" Madge said quickly. After being assured everything was all right, she led the way into the kitchen. Laura immediately decided she was, indeed, going to like Madge Devere. From Gannon's description she had expected someone older, but Madge could hardly be forty, and there was something quite youthful in her manner and pleasant features. She had quick brown eyes, a generous mouth, and dark hair drawn back into a bun. Her figure was still graceful, and she wore her simple but good clothing with a stylish air.

As they headed for the kitchen, Laura glanced through a double door into a parlor that showed Madge Devere's industry—working surfaces were covered with material, shears, tape measures, and a litter of scraps, and on a table in a corner was a rack full of finished hats that made Laura wish for a closer look at Madge's handiwork.

The kitchen was a large, comfortable room, with a huge wood range giving out a welcome warmth after the chill of the spring evening outside. A homey aroma of cooking made Laura realize just how hungry she was. A wooden kitchen table had dishes set for two, and as the visitors were ushered in, a man was putting the silverware in place. He paused and nodded to Frank Gannon. "Hello, Gannon. Just get into town?" he asked, looking in friendly curiosity at the stranger.

As with Madge Devere, Laura felt instinctively that George Howard was a person she was going to like. He was about fifty, clean shaven, with silvering yellow hair and strikingly blue eyes that twinkled at her from behind rimless spectacles. Gannon smiled at the doctor. "Just arrived a few minutes ago. This is Mrs. Kirby. She's from Sacramento, and I suggested she let me bring her to see you."

The doctor raised his brow humorously. "She looks healthy enough to me," he observed, glancing appreciatively at the color the brisk evening had put into her cheeks.

"It's nothing like that," Gannon explained quickly. "I suppose you'd call it a business matter."

"I see." Obviously Dr. Howard did not, but gestured to the chairs. "Why don't we sit down and discuss it?"

Madge Devere spoke up. "Have you folks eaten yet? Everything's ready. Won't you join us?"

Laura shook her head quickly, aware they were interrupting a friendly evening. "Oh, we really couldn't! We didn't drop in like this to have supper!"

The older woman dismissed her refusal with a smile. "Nonsense. It isn't anything special—just stew and biscuits. I always manage to fix too much, and I just have to warm it up again later. You would really be doing me a favor if you'll help us eat it while it's at its best."

Laura gave Gannon a helpless glance, and he grinned. "I think she means it. Personally, I'm too hungry to put up an argument. After all, I've eaten Madge's cooking before."

While the newcomers washed up, two extra places were set. Hungry as she was, Laura could have imagined nothing better than the simple fare: a huge bowl of beef stew, a platter of biscuits with honey, side dishes of slaw and pickled plums, and excellent coffee to wash it all down. Her main concern was to not make a pig of herself, which was not easy since Madge piled her plate high and Laura was feeling starved.

Sitting in the pleasant room, in the company of people who were obviously the best of friends, and listening to their relaxed conversation, Laura's secret anxiety lessened a little. Dr. Howard asked about their journey from Placerville, and Gannon briefly told of their brush with highwaymen and the wounding of his driver.

"Which brings us to Mrs. Kirby," he added, "and the reason I told her she ought to talk to you. When we got to Genoa, Barney Powers needed a doctor but there wasn't any, so Mrs. Kirby volunteered to help. Without anything really to work with, she took care of the bullet wound in a way that I honestly don't think you could have bettered, Doc."

"Is that a fact?" Dr. Howard asked, looking at the young woman with new interest.

"She told me she used to work with her father, a doctor in Sacramento," Gannon went on. "From what I saw, she learned a lot from him. And I thought of the times I've heard you say you wished you had someone you could count on to help you out and be able to take care of emergencies when you had to leave the office. It seems to me you could do a lot worse than to put her on your payroll."

Dr. Howard put down his fork, frowning slightly as

he studied Laura through his spectacles. Laura saw the doubt in his glance. "I admit I was thinking more in terms of—"

"Another doctor?" Laura suggested. "A man?"

"Yes—to be honest," Dr. Howard said uncomfortably.

"*Honest?*" Madge Devere repeated, tossing her head. "I think it's shameful!"

Dr. Howard looked at her. Suddenly put on the defensive, he exclaimed, "What I mean is, any other suggestion just never came up before!" He turned back to Laura. "No offense—please! I never meant to imply that you weren't as good as Frank says—or that I would think you weren't deserving of a chance, just because you happen to be a woman."

"That's all right," Laura said quickly, and tried to mean it. "I hardly expected any other reaction."

"Let me ask you this, Mrs. Kirby. Would you happen to know anything about keeping accounts?"

"Why, naturally. That was always part of my job," she replied.

"Believe me, it's *one* thing I never knew any male doctor to get the hang of. Half the time I can't tell whether I'm getting rich or going broke working my head off," Dr. Howard said ruefully.

"Sounds to me you're talking yourself into the idea," Gannon put in. "One way if not another, she ought to be worth whatever pay you can afford."

"I'm thinking about it," his friend admitted. "I seriously am."

"Thank you," Laura said, genuinely meaning it. "I appreciate even being considered."

"Then you consider real hard, George," Madge told him firmly as she rose and started collecting empty dishes. Laura began to help but was waved back into her chair. "I've baked a dried apple pie that didn't turn out too bad," Madge said. "Would anyone care for a slice? And more coffee to finish off?"

Without waiting for their responses, she brought

out the pie and cut it, refilling everyone's cup from the coffee pot simmering on the stove. As Madge resumed her place, Gannon turned to Laura. "I was just thinking it might help to have some idea how long you might be wanting this job." He turned to George Howard. "Mrs. Kirby's expecting her husband, and I'm not sure what her plans are after that—whether they'll be staying in Carson City or leaving right away."

This was the moment Laura had been secretly dreading all during the meal. As their curious looks settled on her, she could feel the knot inside start to tighten once again as it had while she stood outside the stagecoach with no place to go. Laying down her fork, she forced herself to face Frank Gannon.

"I want to apologize," she said. "I'm afraid I haven't been strictly honest with you."

"Oh?" he said curiously, but she saw his face change. Some of the warmth and friendliness left his eyes. "What do you mean?" he asked.

Laura swallowed. Suddenly she knew this was going to be far worse than she had thought it would be, but she plunged ahead. "Traveling alone like that—surrounded by strange men—I had to be very careful how I answered any questions. I decided it was best to give the impression that I was on my way to meet my husband. I thought I'd be less likely to have trouble than if I admitted I was only coming here to *search* for him. I do hope you understand," she finished rather lamely.

"I think I understand pretty good!" Gannon said briefly.

Appalled at what she heard in his voice, Laura knew she was handling things badly. Madge Devere immediately spoke up in her support. "Any woman would have done exactly the same, my dear. It wouldn't be safe, or necessary, for a woman alone to discuss her personal affairs with just anybody she happened to meet on the road."

Laura thanked her with a quick smile, but a glance

at Frank Gannon showed all too clearly the stiffness that had come into his face. Plainly he was both offended and hurt by her lack of confidence in him, by being treated like someone against whom she had felt she needed to protect herself.

But the damage was done, and it was probably too late to make him believe the truth, Laura thought with regret. Actually she had sensed from the first time she saw him that she would be able to trust Gannon. But to avoid possible problems with the other passengers, she felt she would have to stay with the same story she had already told the others. With dismay Laura realized anything she tried to say now probably would only make matters worse. Perhaps just because she was so anxious, every word she spoke seemed to be coming out wrong.

Draining off his coffee and pushing back his dessert plate, Dr. Howard said, "I don't want to butt in, but do you feel like discussing this now? I take it your husband is missing. If so, and you have reason to think he might be in this area—well, in my line of work I run into quite a lot of people."

"I suppose you would," Laura agreed, grateful for a chance to change the conversation. "The fact is, I haven't heard anything from Jim in months—almost a year. Things hadn't been going so well for him in Sacramento, and he made up his mind to try his luck here in the Washoe country. He thought it was a chance to make a stake. At first he wrote me regularly. Then, after several months, the letters suddenly stopped, and I haven't heard from him since."

Laura sighed and looked down at her hands, which were tightly clasped in her lap. "I wanted to come then," she explained. "But my mother had taken ill—a return of the malaria she caught during the Panama crossing when we came to California in the Gold Rush when I was a very little girl. It was out of the question for me to leave until she was well enough to get along without me."

Dr. Howard was listening solemnly, chewing at the inside of his lower lip thoughtfully. "Jim Kirby?" he repeated slowly. "I'm afraid I don't know the name." He looked across the table at Gannon, who shook his head. "You understand," the older man went on, "an awful lot of men have been pouring into Nevada during the past five years, all bound on making their fortunes. Very few actually do. That's the nature of these mining booms. But it would be awfully hard to track down any one individual, unless there's something pretty definite to go on."

"What about letters?" Madge suggested. "What could they tell you?"

"Most of them seem to have been sent from a place called Aurora," Laura said.

"Oh, yes. I know that camp." The doctor nodded. "I've been there. It's about a hundred miles south of here. At one time it was pretty lively, but there's not much doing there now. You could go down there, of course, and poke around. But I don't like to think of you trying it alone."

"I've come this far by myself. Now that I'm here I can't give up without making an effort," Laura said determinedly. "Maybe I'll be lucky."

Madge reached across the table and patted Laura's hand with a reassuring smile. George Howard cleared his throat and continued. "I was going to say that I expect to be heading down that way myself, one day next week. If you can wait that long, I'll be glad to take you with me and see what we're able to scare up. And while you're waiting," he added, "if you really think you'd like to take a try as my assistant—well, the job is yours. What's more, if it turns out you're able to do a man's work, looks only fair to me that you should also get his pay."

Madge Devere clapped her hands together and smiled broadly. "Now, that makes sense," she declared. "Good for you, George." She turned to Laura. "What's

more, I think you'll find he isn't too bad a fellow to
work with."

"Why, thank you," Laura exclaimed, smiling at
Dr. Howard. "Thank you both." Then, a little uncertainly, she looked at Gannon. "And you, too, Mr.
Gannon—for suggesting it in the first place." Laura had
a dismal impression that he was still angry at her.

"Glad to be of help," was all he said. "Now it looks
like you'll have to think about finding a place to stay.
Maybe these good people will have some ideas on that,
too." Pushing back his chair, he got abruptly to his feet.
"I'm afraid I have to be leaving. I'm due at the Overland office for a meeting." He quickly thanked Madge
for supper and said a brief goodnight. And then he was
gone.

Laura had risen, too, vainly searching for words to
try and explain why she had not told Gannon the truth
during her trip. She stood helpless as Gannon's footsteps echoed down the carpeted hallway. The street
door opened and closed again, then there was silence.

"What in the world do you suppose is the matter
with *him*? That didn't sound a bit like Frank Gannon!"
Madge exclaimed.

"I'm afraid I know," Laura told her. "It's because
he found out I lied to him."

"But you explained all that," Dr. Howard protested.
"He surely understood your reasons."

"I don't know," Laura said unhappily. "I think he's
convinced I deliberately meant to be rude, while he
only wanted to help me if he could. Now it's come to
this—and it makes me feel terrible!"

Madge put an arm on Laura's shoulder. "Well,
don't let it," she said firmly. "Frank's proud and he's
sensitive. But he's not unreasonable. Give him time,
he'll get over this. Meanwhile I'm thinking of that last
thing he said. Do you have a place to stay?"

"I'm afraid I hadn't actually thought that far ahead.
I suppose a hotel—or a room somewhere."

The older woman had a sudden inspiration. "Why

not stay here? I mean it," she insisted before Laura could say anything. "Look, I've got this whole house, and nobody but me living in it."

Dr. Howard stared. "Madge, you've never taken in roomers."

"No, somehow it never occurred to me. And I wouldn't take just anyone. But I get lonesome, sometimes, and it might be nice having a body on the place I can talk to. I already know the two of us would get along fine. Let me at least show you my spare room," she urged Laura. "Then you can make up your mind."

Looking into the woman's friendly face, Laura decided instantly. "I think I've already made up my mind. I'd love to stay with you."

"Good!" Madge cried. "Your things are already here. You can move right in."

Chapter 4

By the time Gannon reached the Overland office, he had managed to work off much of his resentment and disappointment. He told himself he had no right to blame Laura Kirby. Young and attractive and on her own, she had only been smart to treat every man she met with caution, using any method to hold them at arm's length—Frank Gannon included. He supposed it was simply his male ego that was affronted, because she had not seen at once he was no threat to her, but rather a man of decency who only wished her well.

It really did not matter, anyway. He had been glad to help her get her feet under her in this unfamiliar place. If he was just as skeptical as Dr. Howard about her chances of tracing her husband, it was really none of his business. She was another man's wife and already he had interfered in her life as much as he had any right to.

But it was not easy to forget her. Laura Kirby had made a strong impression on him. Gannon forced himself to put her from his mind as he approached the stage-line office and the confrontation that he knew awaited him.

At once he saw the coach that had been unhitched and parked in the work area beside the station. He stopped for a moment to look at it by the light from an oil lantern hung on a pole. The coach was famous the length of the Overland trail that stretched from the Missouri River to California. Ben Holladay had had it custom built, to his own specifications. Instead of the clumsy leather thoroughbraces on which the ordinary Concord stagecoach was slung, this one had coil springs that would absorb the shock of the roughest road. Though Gannon had never looked inside, he understood it contained all the necessary equipment for an office on wheels, including a writing desk and even an easily made up bed. It was in this coach that the boss of the Overland stage line made his twice-yearly inspection tours over the entire length of his farflung empire. Gannon straightened his shoulders and said aloud, "Well—here goes!" He walked through the splashes of lamplight from the station windows, mounted a couple of steps, and pushed open the door. He found two men waiting for him. "Good evening, Ben . . . Merl," he said.

Ben Holladay was seated at Gannon's own desk, with whiskey and glasses in front of him and a halo of cigar smoke above his head. A solid figure of a man in his early forties, his bearded features bore a certain resemblance to General Ulysses Grant. His manner was direct and invited no nonsense.

He returned Gannon's greeting with a nod, while the second man, who had been studying a wall map showing the entire western section of the Overland stage route, slowly turned for a long look at Gannon before saying sternly, "Well, *here* you are! I'd about decided you were planning not to show up."

Gannon met the man's cold stare levelly. "I was in a while earlier and left word I'd be back. Didn't you get the message?"

Ben Holladay gestured impatiently with one hand. "Sure, we got it." He sounded in a more tolerant mood. "We haven't been waiting long. You're well, are you, Frank?"

"Well enough. How was your trip from Missouri?"

"Hit a late snowstorm in the Rockies. Otherwise, it was fairly monotonous. At least the Indians are quiet and leaving our stations alone—a big change from last year." Holladay indicated a chair opposite him. "Sit down. Help yourself to the booze, Frank, and let's talk."

Gannon seated himself and took the bottle of the special brand Holladay always carried with him. Pouring a spare inch of whiskey into his glass, Gannon set the bottle aside and let the drink stand, untasted. He waited, watching the others.

The second man, Merl Lunsford, stood with arms folded, his expression one of thinly veiled hostility. Gannon had not realized Holladay was bringing Lunsford along, from division headquarters in Salt Lake City. As the superintendent in charge of the western third of the route, Lunsford was Gannon's immediate superior. Under his direction, Gannon was responsible for the last stretch of the route, between Virginia City and the end of the line, at Placerville. Ultimately, of course, Ben Holladay kept a firm hand on every phase of the whole operation.

For reasons that were not entirely clear to Gannon, there had been a certain amount of hostility between himself and Lunsford for the entire six months since Gannon had taken over his new position. During the time he had worked hard, trying to turn in a job that would do credit to the division and to his superiors, and yet the friction had remained. Lunsford, an efficient administrator, had never seemed a spiteful man. His continuing attitude both puzzled and bothered Gannon. Perhaps the trouble was that Holladay, in his own direct way, had promoted Gannon to division agent himself, without consulting Merl Lunsford. If so, it had not made Gannon's job any easier.

Holladay settled back in his chair with a cigar between his fingers and whiskey within reach. "Shall we get down to business?" he began. "It looks like this division has a new problem since my last trip. I want to hear the details."

"I've never held anything back. I've made full and complete reports to Lunsford," Gannon stated quickly.

"Which he has passed on to me," Holladay said,

nodding. "But let's go over it again, in case I might have forgotten or overlooked something. It's not an entirely new situation," he went on. "We've always had a fair amount of trouble along this stretch, ever since the big silver strikes brought the boomers in by the thousands, looking to hit it rich. Most didn't, of course. And later some of them were apt to find the idea of holding up a stagecoach more tempting than a job of hard work at day wages."

Merl Lunsford snorted. "Amateurs! Petty thieves! No reason why *anyone* couldn't cope with riffraff like that."

It was a direct dig at Gannon, but he refused to rise to it. It was Holladay who answered. "I put Gannon in charge of this section because he had driven stagecoaches through here and knew every mile of it. And because I thought he was capable. Nothing has happened so far to make me decide I was wrong." He looked at his division agent. "What do *you* say about this, Frank?"

"I say these are no amateurs we're dealing with. This is a gang at work. Well led, well organized, and knowing just what they're after. When they hit one of our stages it's always planned in such a way as to take our men off guard, with no real chance for resistance," Gannon explained. "They've shot up our relay stations and run our team horses out of the corrals and got away scot free. Last week they raised the ante: A wagon hauling supplies for us was waylaid and the driver set afoot. The raiders took whatever they wanted and burned the rest—along with the wagon. So far all of this doesn't seem to add up, but one of these days I suppose we'll begin to see the sense of it."

Holladay pulled at his lower lip as he listened to Gannon, nodding grimly as the reports from the field were confirmed. "I also understand they've hit the telegraph between here and Placerville," he said.

"That's correct. Almost as soon as the cut was spliced they did it again. And the second time, they

used an old Indian trick. They took out a few inches of
the wire and replaced it with a piece of rawhide, so the
break was all but impossible to spot from the ground. If
the repair crew hadn't found it by pure luck, they'd be
out there hunting it yet."

Holladay gestured impatiently with the fuming stub
of his cigar. "That's the telegraph company's problem.
We've got enough of our own. The point is, do you
have any proof that this was all the work of the same
bunch of men?"

"No," Gannon admitted. "But it has the same smell."

"We need more than speculation!" his employer
said roughly. "I thought you actually nabbed one of
them, and were hoping to make him talk. Did anything
come of that? Or was it a false alarm?"

"We have a prisoner," Gannon explained. "A man
named Bart Kramer. He was shot and left behind by his
friends in a holdup that didn't quite come off. From the
way that particular job was bungled, it could have been
the work of amateurs and not the gang we're talking
about. But Kramer turned out to be tough enough.
Nobody could get a word out of him, not even when
the judge promised a lighter sentence in return for
information on the rest of the outlaws. We never learned
anything at all."

"Where is he now?" Holladay asked, reaching for
his whiskey.

"He's sitting in a cell out at the prison—still keeping his mouth shut," Gannon replied. "But it looks as
though we might not have him much longer. There's a
sheriff from California in town with the papers to take
Kramer back with him to hang for an old murder charge.
We could try fighting it, of course, but I doubt it would
do any good. California obviously has a higher claim.
And after all, the man has already been given every
chance to talk, assuming that he even knows anything."

Merl Lunsford broke in impatiently. "You've been
giving us ancient history! We want to know what happens next. Just what are you doing about this, Gannon?

Some time ago you were given authority to hire enough extra guards to protect our shipments and the stage line's property. Have you hired them yet?"

"Not as many as I need," Gannon admitted.

"Why not?" Lunsford snapped.

Gannon struggled to hold his temper. "If I merely wanted to hire a lot of guns—and do it fast—I could pick them up in any bar on Carson Street. But who knows what kind of men they would be? I have to screen them as best I can, and that takes time. Otherwise the gang we're fighting could plant their own men on us where they could do us the most harm."

"A valid point," Ben Holladay agreed. "We can't afford not to be careful." He scowled for a moment, rolling the cigar between his jaws. "What was it we heard about one of your drivers getting shot today and nearly killed?"

"It was a sniper," Gannon confirmed. "On the road south of Genoa. As it turned out, the wound was shallow and not too serious. But it could have been. I happened to be riding the box, and I'm not sure which of the two of us the sniper really was aiming at."

"Could have been somebody with a grudge against you, you mean?" Holladay asked.

"Maybe. Or maybe they had me spotted, knew my job with the company, and thought by knocking me off the box they could disrupt things some more while you were choosing my replacement." Gannon had a question of his own he wanted to ask, but hesitated for a moment, not knowing how the other man would take it. He decided to go ahead. "How about yourself? Is it possible you might have some personal enemies?"

Holladay shot Gannon a stabbing look as he reached for his whiskey. "Are you serious? A man like me— *enemies*?" He gave a short laugh. "Hell! You'll find them under every rock between here and the Missouri River! A man who gets too big too fast can figure on it. So you think it's really me they're after, do you? Hitting at me through my stage line?"

"The thought occurred to me," Gannon said.

Ben Holladay drained his glass. "It doesn't matter," he said firmly. "It'll take more than this to stop the Overland! Hell, last season it was the Paiutes. Hardly one of our stations between Virginia City and Salt Lake that they didn't hit. But even so the stages kept rolling. And nobody needs to think different now, unless they come up with something a lot worse than they've thrown at us so far!"

He set down his glass and peered at the man across the desk. "One final question. Just how sure are you of the men you have under you?"

Gannon's mouth tightened, and he tried to keep the anger from his voice. "Do you mean, are they to be trusted? Ben, I *know* these men. I've worked right alongside them for months. If you think any one of them might be capable of selling you out and selling out the Overland—I'm willing to stake my job that you're dead wrong!"

The older man studied him for a long moment, then nodded. "I happen to be of the same opinion. I just wanted to hear it from you. Very well," he added crisply. "I consider this to have been a successful meeting. Finish your drink." It was an order, as well as a sign that the meeting was concluded. With some relief that it had proved less of an ordeal than he had expected, Gannon drained his glass.

Merl Lunsford was not satisfied at all. He had been silently leaning against the wall where a bracket lamp cast deep shadows across his gaunt features. Suddenly he straightened and took a step forward in quick protest. "That was *it*?" he exclaimed to Holladay. "That's all we came here for? Hell, we haven't settled anything! We haven't made a single move toward cleaning up the mess this section has got itself into!"

There was no question how he had hoped to see that accomplished. The unspoken words "by firing Frank Gannon" plainly hovered in the air. The baleful stare he shot Gannon said it vividly. But Holladay seemed unaffected by the outburst. "No one's going to perform any miracles overnight," he said calmly. "As I see it, we can only hang tight until we're able to build up the manpower we need to do this job properly." He turned to Gannon. "I depend on you to hold things together. Merl and I will be going on to Placerville and from there to San Francisco for a meeting with some of the head men at Wells Fargo. While we're there I have sources that should be able to supply us with all the additional, reliable men we need. Also I plan to talk to the military about army escorts for our stages. I'm not too optimistic about that. The war in Virginia has got the army stretched thin by now. I expect to be told we're going to have to shift for ourselves. Well, we'll see. For now, we seem to have settled our business in Carson City," he added, getting to his feet.

"Are we leaving right away?" Merl Lunsford wanted to know.

Holladay shook his head. "It's getting on, and I think I'd enjoy spending a night in a hotel bed for once. But I want us to be ready to go at first light."

"Whatever you say." Lunsford definitely sounded relieved. He found Holladay's normal style of travel—day and night, almost without stopping—something of a trial, even in the comfort of the specially constructed coach.

Holladay turned to Gannon. "I need a relief driver to take over the coach tomorrow. Would Hank Monk happen to be in town?"

"He should be. Shall I get him?" Gannon asked.

"Not Monk!" Lunsford echoed the name in horror. "That drunkard?"

Gannon had been determined not to start any quarrels, but he automatically spoke up. "Drunk or sober, Hank is a top driver, the best I've ever seen in action. And I've seen him when he had to be carried out and set on the box. But once those reins are in his hands, he can outdrive any of the rest of us!"

Lunsford started to retort. "That's neither here nor—"

But Holladay broke in with a chuckle. "Old Horace Greeley still tells about the ride he took with Hank Monk across the Sierras from here, back in fifty-nine. He made the mistake of saying he was in a hurry to reach Placerville, so Monk allowed that they'd hurry some. He made the whole distance in ten hours flat, and Greeley presented him with a gold watch to remember the occasion. We aren't in that big a hurry," he told Gannon. "But get me Hank. Say I want him bright and early, and preferably sober. Though maybe that would be too much to ask for."

Gannon nodded. "I'll see to it."

Lunsford looked a little apprehensive, but he knew better than to protest anymore. He said glumly, "I'll fetch our bags out of the coach and see they're taken to the hotel." Without looking at Gannon, he left the office.

Watching him go, Holladay said with amusement, "No need for him to know Horace Greeley told me he actually gave Hank that watch out of sheer gratitude for still being alive! But if I've got a choice, Hank's the one I want. I'll feel sure, with him up there on the seat."

"What about a guard?" Gannon asked.

Holladay shook his head. "It's taken care of. I brought a good man with me."

"You sure one will be enough? I don't want to see anything go wrong tomorrow."

"With Hank Monk holding the reins, I figure we'll leave any kind of trouble eating our dust!" Turning back to the desk, he drew some papers from his pocket. "I have a couple of letters to get out. I better get started on them."

"All right, Ben. I'll go locate Hank and see you in the morning, if not before."

Gannon had scarcely stepped outside when he saw something odd going on in Holladay's special coach. A door stood wide open, and from inside came muffled voices and the sounds of a scuffle. Alarmed, Gannon ran for the coach.

Despite the glow of a nearby lantern, it was impossible to make out exactly what was happening, but as he approached, two men suddenly came tumbling out. When they broke apart Gannon saw that one was Merl Lunsford, who had just hauled a second man out of the coach. The second man had missed the high step and sprawled on the ground. Lunsford hauled the man to his feet and shoved him, hard, against the side of the vehicle, where the stranger stood swaying slightly, offering no resistance.

"What seems to be the trouble!" Gannon exclaimed.

Lunsford threw him the briefest of angry looks. "Where's your sheriff?" he demanded harshly. "I want this man arrested. He's been violating private property!"

The evicted man drew himself up. "Violating?" he repeated indignantly. "Sir, I'll ask you to watch your language!"

"What would *you* call what you were doing?"

"I kind of think that I was taking a nap," the man said carefully and a shade uncertainly.

"But nobody can do that in Mr. Holladay's private coach!" Lunsford said indignantly.

"Oh, on the contrary! It was quite comfortable. I dropped right off!"

In the lantern light, the man looked to be in his late twenties, of medium height, with a heavy red mustache and a tousled mop of red hair. Gannon sighed and shook his head. "Sam, are you drunk again?"

The man gave the question his full attention. "Do you know, I was beginning to wonder about that," he finally said slowly.

Still angry, and breathing hard from dragging his prisoner into the open, Lunsford turned to Gannon. "Are you acquainted with this fellow?"

"Sure." The whole affair struck Gannon as amusing, but it seemed unwise to laugh at the moment. "This is Sam Clemens. He's harmless. He's a newspaperman.

Works on the *Territorial Enterprise*, up at Virginia City."

Lunsford's distaste showed in his expression and the tone of his voice. "A reporter! I always did consider them to be a breed of drunken louts! I've a mind to make an example of this one."

"But, why? He didn't do anything so bad, did he?" Gannon asked. "Everybody's heard about this special coach. Sam probably got word that Ben Holladay was in town, and when he saw it parked here I imagine he couldn't resist the chance to try it out for himself. I've thought I'd like to, more than once."

Lunsford shook his head, adamantly. "If we were to let every Tom, Dick, and Harry—"

"Hold it just a minute." Gannon turned to the reporter with a warning. "Sam, you're to stay right where you are, understand? Don't even move."

"I'm flattered," Sam Clemens mumbled. "What makes you think I could?" Gannon took Lunsford by an elbow and drew him aside. He spoke quietly and earnestly. "I know how you feel about this. But if you make an issue of it and have him thrown in jail, you'll bring trouble on yourself and on Holladay, too. Believe me—sober, Sam Clemens is one of the funniest and, when he wants to be, one of the cruelest writers anybody ever read. I promise you, he'll make a story out of this that will turn you into the laughingstock of the territory. He'll crucify you—and there'd be not a damn thing you could do about it!"

But Lunsford remained stubborn, and Gannon reluctantly played his final card. "All right," he said bluntly. "If that's not enough, think about this. Apparently you're not aware that Sam's brother, Orion Clemens, is the secretary of state here in Nevada and is also serving right now as acting governor."

As he had supposed it would, that information had its effect. Lunsford's face went blank.

"Are you telling me the truth?" he demanded suspiciously.

"Every word."

A man who greatly respected power in any form, political or otherwise, Lunsford swore and with a shrug said heavily, "Take the man, will you? Just get him away from here!"

"Right now," Gannon said. He turned back to the coach, where the object of the controversy was waiting as he had been told. "Come along, Sam," Gannon said, taking the reporter's arm. "I want to talk to you." Merl Lunsford looked after them, scowling, as the two men left the stage yard.

Chapter 5

Even when sober Sam Clemens was not particularly impressive. He was given to slovenliness, his clothing and his person not always clean. Gannon had heard Clemens describe himself as looking like an untended grave. Some of the reporter's enemies said much worse—that he was shiftless, malicious, untruthful, and a cadger who had never been known to buy a drink himself.

But Gannon liked Clemens and admired the wry quickness of his mind. Though he almost never told anything the same way twice, Gannon knew Clemens had come west from Hannibal, Missouri, three years before—to avoid being drafted into the Union army, his enemies said. His brother Orion having somehow wrangled a political appointment, Sam had hoped to work for his brother but there was no money for a salary. So instead he had hung around the mining camps and tried prospecting. But daily labor with a pick and shovel was distasteful and he had not found any silver.

As a last resort he had sent some humorous letters to the Virginia City paper, written in the style of such backwoods humorists as Artemus Ward and Petroleum V. Nasby. This had led to the offer of a job more to Clemens's liking, one with little physical work attached. Approaching thirty, he seemed to have no ambition at all beyond turning out wildly extravagant nonsense under his chosen pseudonym of "Mark Twain," playing practical jokes on his friends among the *Enterprise* staff, and carrying on a highly publicized feud with the publisher of a rival Virginia City newspaper.

49

As Gannon and Clemens walked through the chill of the spring night, the reporter said, "I guess I have to thank you for getting rid of that fellow back there. He was certainly a noisy sonofabitch! I just wasn't in any mood to argue with him."

"Didn't look to me you were in any shape to argue," Gannon said sternly. "Don't you think it was a poor place you chose to sleep it off?"

"You got it wrong!" Clemens protested. "That was in the line of duty—field work."

"Then maybe you better think about getting into a less dangerous occupation," Gannon suggested.

"Look, my friend, I still bear the marks of the trip I took coming out here on the Overland, three years ago," Clemens explained earnestly. "Talk about roughing it! They half filled the coaches with mail sacks, and we had to climb in on top of them. God, that was lumpy! Well, tonight, in the name of honest journalism, I saw a chance to make a comparison with the style in which the great Holladay does his traveling."

"And instead you spoiled everything by going to sleep. One drink too many, I suppose?"

"There's no such thing as one drink too many," Clemens insisted.

"Have it your way," Gannon shrugged and changed the subject. "Have you seen Hank Monk?"

"Lots of times."

"I meant, this evening," Gannon said patiently.

"Oh." Clemens dug his blunt fingers into his tousled red hair, trying to remember. "It could be," he said finally. "Or was it last night? I see him in the saloon so often, it's hard to say."

"All right, thanks. I'll drop around and see if I can find him," Gannon said, starting off. Clemens tagged along. "Wait for me. I'm on the verge of feeling thirsty again."

"Sure, come along. I'll buy you one," Gannon offered.

When they entered the bar the first person Gannon

spotted, in the glow of oil lamps shining murkily through clouds of stale tobacco smoke, was the man he wanted. "Bull's-eye!" he told his companion. He tossed a coin on the bar, caught the bartender's eye, and jerked a thumb at Clemens. As the drink was being poured, Gannon picked his way through the crowd to where Hank Monk sat alone at a back table, a whiskey bottle at his elbow.

A man in his early thirties, with curly black hair and a black mustache and spade beard, Hank Monk had a wealth of yarns that could always entertain an audience when he was in a mood for talking. However, as Gannon approached he saw the driver staring straight ahead, a glass held loosely in his hand. He showed no reaction when Gannon dropped into a chair beside him.

"Hank?" Gannon touched the man on the shoulder. "This is Gannon. Can you hear me?"

The driver's head turned, but his eyes were vague and unfocused. "I hear you. But I don't *see* you too good."

"That's all right," Gannon said. "All I want from you now is to listen. You got a job to do. Ben Holladay is in town, and he's asked for you, by name. Wants you to take him and Merl Lunsford to California in that coach of his. You think you'll be in shape by morning?"

Hank Monk considered the idea seriously. "I'll work on it."

"I take that to mean 'yes.' Now, pay attention, Hank," Gannon insisted. "Holladay is on serious business, and he won't be wanting to waste any time. But for God's sake, I don't want you to try to earn yourself another gold watch! Is that clear?"

The driver looked disappointed. But he finally nodded, "Oh, all right."

"One more thing that ought to be obvious enough that I don't have to spell it out. You'll have an armed guard along. Even so, if certain people were to catch on that Ben Holladay is in that coach, they might be of a mind to make real trouble. So be especially careful."

Monk peered thoughtfully into his glass, which seemed to have emptied itself somehow. He picked up the bottle and said, "The last time anybody tried to stop a coach I was driving, I bounced one of these off his skull. Never had any trouble since. But I always make it a point to carry plenty of ammunition." He weighed the bottle in his palm, testing its heft.

Gannon, who knew the story about the outlaw and the bottle, pushed his chair back and said, "Fine. Could be several days before you get back. Ben's talking about going on clear to San Francisco, then coming back to Carson City with some new guards. At any rate, you just see that you're at the station and ready to roll by first light. If you aren't, I'll be coming to look for you!"

As he was leaving, he passed the bar and saw a knot of men gathered about Sam Clemens and laughing uproariously over something he had just said. One of the men hailed Gannon with an invitation to a drink. "Thanks, I can't," Gannon said. "I'm just in from California. Have to get back to the office and find out how big a pile of work has been collecting for me while I was away."

As he turned to go, someone called after him. "You're a good influence for me," Sam Clemens said when he reached Gannon. "And you don't know how much I hate it! You've just reminded me that I have a story to work up. I better go do it before my notes get so cold I can't read them."

"Sorry to do that to you," Gannon said with a grin. "I suppose you're staying at your brother's? I'll walk part way."

As they moved into the evening chill, a newcomer stepped up onto the porch. Light from the door behind them showed it was Sheriff Linus Fox. "Well, my extradition papers are all signed and legal," the lawman told Gannon. "It's given me quite a runaround. It seems your governor is back east somewhere, and so I had to locate the acting governor. That turned out to be the secretary of state, a fellow named Orion Clemens. I tracked him down where he lives, and—" He broke off abruptly, staring blankly at Gannon's companion.

"This is his brother, Sam," Gannon said and made the introductions.

As the two men shook hands, Fox asked, "Did anyone ever tell you, you Clemenses look just alike?"

"You noticed that?" the reporter commented with a straight face. "Actually, Orion's quite a bit older. But everybody who sees us thinks one of us has just got to be a twin. Trouble is, they never can decide which one of us it is."

"Don't let Sam confuse you," Gannon warned, seeing the sheriff's expression as he tried to work it out. "He loves confusing people. He writes for the paper at Virginia City, and when readers see the name Mark Twain they know they're going to have their legs pulled."

Sheriff Fox gave a start. "Mark Twain?" he echoed. "Hell, I've heard *that* name! I know it well!"

"I deny everything!" Clemens retorted stoutly. "I've never even *been* to California."

"Maybe you haven't. But our papers are starting to pick up your articles and run them, and everybody I know keeps his eyes open for the next one. Personally, I think they're funny as hell!"

Gannon was puzzled by Clemens's reaction to this unexpected praise. It was impossible to tell whether his friend was pleased, or angry, or simply embarrassed. For once Sam Clemens was at a loss for words. He scowled, his thick brows lowered, and the red mustache bristled. In the end he shrugged and muttered roughly, "Must be hard up for something to read!" Without another word he turned abruptly and walked down the saloon's steps, vanishing into the night.

"That's a strange fellow," the sheriff grunted.

Gannon agreed. "For a fact." Wanting to change the subject, he asked, "So when do you pick up Bart Kramer?"

"Tomorrow, early as possible. I want to get away with him on the morning stage if I can." Linus Fox hesitated, seeming troubled, then blurted out, "I hope you understand, I'm only doing my job. I feel kind of bad about this. But the storekeeper he murdered was well thought of. I'd have a hard time explaining things if I was to go home without Kramer."

Gannon shrugged. "You might as well take him. Since we haven't pried anything out of him so far, I don't see that we ever will. The man's been just too tough for us. By the same token, I advise you not to take any chances with him."

"I'll keep it in mind." The sheriff held out his hand. "If I don't happen to see you again before I leave, good luck to you." Gannon took the hand and they shook briefly.

The next morning, as Sheriff Fox drove down the road going east from Carson City, he noticed the odd color to the sky and decided that a storm could very well be on the way. Scudding clouds hid the crests of the hills behind the town, and a steady wind combed the sage of the valley flat. The wind made the canvas top of the rented buggy crack like pistol shots and caused the horse to toss its head uneasily. Fox turned up the collar of his coat.

After a couple of miles the prison where Bart Kramer was being held came into sight. The sheriff had been told what to look for, a single cavernous stone building, with a flimsy wooden roof, a rock quarry nearby, and a scatter of sheds and outhouses.

There was little sign of life, except for a rhythmic clang of metal that must have come from the prison blacksmith shop and drifts of woodsmoke rising from a number of chimneys. As Fox halted his rig, a guard armed with a rifle came out to challenge him. The guard looked at the papers identifying the sheriff and explaining his mission. After asking some suspicious questions and scrutinizing Acting Governor Clemens's signature, Fox was permitted past the guard and into a tiny partitioned office. Inside the office the prison warden, a heavy-set, scowling man named Smith took his time reading through the extradition document. Fox stood and looked at the wall behind the warden's chair, which had been lined with canvas covered by cheap wallpaper. He could see it billowing faintly as the wind pushed through the chinks in the uncemented stone.

The chair creaked protestingly under Warden Smith as he leaned back, tossing the papers onto the cheap pine table that served as a desk. He gave the sheriff a piercing look. "So you want Bart Kramer? Well, you won't get any argument from me! Far as I'm concerned you're welcome to the bastard. He's given me nothing but trouble. I swear, he's little more than an animal. All I ask is that you take him and see he's hanged. I sure as hell never want him back here."

"I wouldn't worry," Sheriff Fox assured him. "I'll have him off your hands."

The warden pulled open a drawer and rummaged through it looking for the form he needed. "The prisoners are eating breakfast," he said. "While you sign this receipt I'll have him got ready." As Fox signed, the warden went to open the door of the guard room. "Good news!" he called to the man on duty. "We're getting rid of Bart Kramer. Give him some clothes, and fetch him here to me," he ordered before returning to his seat.

While they waited Fox admitted to the warden he was not looking forward to his return trip by stagecoach across the Sierras with a prisoner, even though such things were routine inconveniences for a law officer.

Suddenly the guard returned—alone. "Looks like they been having some trouble, Chief!" he reported excitedly.

"What kind of trouble?"

"That sonofabitch Kramer! He's still in his cell—said he wasn't going to spend another day in that quarry, and he refused to come out."

The warden bristled. "Oh, did he? He's not that tough. Why didn't the boys just go in and drag him out?"

"I understand Harry Riling told them not to. He said not to bother you about it, either. Said he'd get Kramer out his own way. Then he ordered the rest of the prisoners marched off to breakfast and he locked the door of Kramer's cell and went out to the blacksmith shop. To get something, he said. I guess he's still out there. And Kramer's setting tight."

"Oh, hell!" Warden Smith slapped a meaty palm on his desk and pushed himself to his feet. "It's always something in this damned rathole of a prison! Still, I can usually count on Harry Riling to think of a way to keep the scum in line. I guess I better go see what it is this time."

Sheriff Fox followed the warden and the guard through a door into the cellblock that occupied the middle section of the long building. Inside it was dark, cold, and raked by chilling drafts leaking in through a honeycomb of chinks in the crude construction. The grilled doors of tiny cells lined either side of a narrow hallway. Beyond another doorway, a confusion of voices and the rattle of metal utensils marked the dining room, where the inmates were being fed their morning meal.

All the cell doors but one stood open. Through the grill of cell number five, Sheriff Fox glimpsed the face of a man. A guard in a uniform and billed cap stood peering in at the prisoner. The guard, Fox thought, might be Harry Riling. Thin and wiry, with the foxy, narrow features of a man who relied on his wits, Riling was talking loudly to the prisoner in a nasal and rasping voice. "All right! You've had a little time to think it over, Kramer. Ready now to play it smart and come out of there?"

There was a rough shout of defiance from within the cell. Riling seemed not at all displeased by the response. "That suits me," he called. "I got something here that'll *pry* you loose!" He brought up a length of iron bar he had with him.

In the dim corridor, Fox saw a dull glow and caught the faintly acrid scent of heated metal. He opened his mouth to protest but the red-hot end of the rod had already been shoved through the grilled opening. The prisoner was driven backward, but he made an instinctive move to grab the rod and knock it aside or wrest it from Riling's grasp. At once there rose an anguished cry from the prisoner.

"Changing your mind, Kramer?" Harry Riling taunted. "Or d'you want more?" He laughed as he prodded at the interior of the tiny cubicle, shifting the glowing bar around, probing with savage thrusts. Cries of fear and agony tumbled through the corridor. Then finally came a broken plea. "Stop it! Oh, God—*stop it!* I'll come out!"

Harry Riling stepped back. He was breathing heavily and grinning broadly as he retorted, "You damn bet you will!"

For the first time Warden Smith moved to interfere. "I think you done the job, Harry. Let it go. Who has the key?" he asked.

Riling withdrew the hot iron from the cell door and tossed it carelessly aside. Fox quickly sidestepped as he felt the heat of the hot prod strike the floor near him. Horrified by such barbarity, he watched in silence as Riling turned the key and swung the heavy door wide. The man who stumbled from the cell was a hulking shape in black and white striped prison garb. He had a shaved head and a wedge-shaped face that was wider at the jaw than at the brow, which was shining with sweat despite the chill of the corridor. Bart Kramer's mouth gaped amid a black stubble of beard. His clothing smoked in several places, and the hands he flung before him had already begun to blister from the hot iron.

The moment he saw Harry Riling the prisoner's face twisted with hatred, and with a shout of rage he hurled himself at his tormentor. Quickly a second guard stepped in, striking Kramer across the chest with his rifle barrel and forcing him back. Kramer stood with chest heaving, glaring at Riling. The door to the dining hall had been thrown open, and two guards were peer-

ing into the corridor to see what was going on. Warden
Smith turned and bellowed angrily. "You! Get back to
your job!" Reluctantly the guards withdrew.

Riling seemed pleased with himself and anxious for
praise. "Guess I learned him never to pull that trick
again—him or anyone else!"

"At least Kramer won't be pulling it here. He's
leaving us," Smith answered. "Getting extradited to
California on a hanging charge. The two of you put
some other clothes on him. I want him out of here fast!"

The warden turned to go, but Bart Kramer held up
his blistered hands and shouted, "Warden! Damn it,
can't you see the sonofabitch fried me?"

Smith flicked him the briefest of looks. "You ain't
hurt," he said, almost in contempt, and continued to
his office.

Sheriff Fox was a man hardened by a tough job,
but nevertheless he was shaken by what he had
witnessed. Falling in with the warden, he demanded
coldly, "Is this how you run your prison?"

"When I have to," Smith answered crisply. "You
may have noticed that things are pretty primitive around
here. We can't afford to let scum like that get away with
anything. When they do get out of line, I count on
Harry Riling to figure out the best medicine. As for
Bart Kramer, now you've seen what he is. You got to be
ready to take the whip to him!"

Fox kept his mouth shut. Talk seemed useless.

At last Kramer was ready for delivery. The striped
prison garb had been exchanged for ill-fitting civilian
clothes that must once have belonged to some other
inmate. As Kramer was marched out and ordered to
take a seat in the buggy, the warden warned Sheriff
Fox, "Never turn your back on him! If you brought
handcuffs, then I advise you to put 'em on him and
keep 'em there."

After a look at Bart Kramer's glowering features,
Sheriff Fox reluctantly decided to take the advice. He
brought out the irons, and at his order the prisoner put

out his wrists. Seeing the blistered flesh of Kramer's palms, Fox took care in snapping the manacles in place. When the rig was heading for Carson City, the lawman felt a need to talk to his prisoner. "I have to say I didn't like what I saw back there. I reckon you've been something shy of a model prisoner, but it was no excuse for that fellow Riling. I take it you had trouble with him before this?"

When he got no answer, he gave the other man a quick look. Bart Kramer was scowling and staring straight ahead. Observing the beetling brows, shapeless features, and sullen expression, Fox remembered Warden Smith's comment, *He's little more than an animal.* But even an animal deserves halfway decent treatment, Fox thought sourly. "Those burns look pretty damn painful," he said. "Soon as we're in town I'll see about having something done for them." Kramer gave no sign that he even heard.

When they arrived in Carson City it was still early, and the streets were nearly empty. Turning north onto Carson Street, they had ridden a couple of blocks before the sheriff reined in the horses and called to a man walking alone on the wooden sidewalk, "Friend, do you know where I might find a doctor?"

The man jerked a thumb over his shoulder. "A block farther, then turn left. Doc Howard's on the north side of the street. You'll see his shingle."

Fox thanked him and drove on. The doctor's place proved to be easy to find, and Fox pulled in, set the brake, and told his prisoner, "Come along. We'll see what this Doc Howard can do about fixing you up." Kramer climbed heavily out of the rig and let himself be led up the path.

Chapter 6

Reporting for the first day of her new job, Laura Kirby had been surprised to find the door unlocked and the office empty. A fire was going in the stove, taking off the morning chill, but though she called out Dr. Howard's name, she got no answer. She stood in the silence of the unfamiliar room, looking about at its sketchy furnishings—a few stiff chairs, a glass-fronted bookcase stuffed with heavy tomes, a framed medical diploma on the wall, and in one corner, a table for emergency operations.

Then she caught sight of a penciled note lying on the rolltop desk, and she went over and picked it up. Under her name it read, in a hurried scrawl, "Sorry, but I've been called to set a broken leg, with a couple of other calls to make after that. But I'm sure you can hold the fort alone while I'm gone. Signed: G.H."

"I don't know why not," Laura said aloud and went to hang up her hat and coat.

The first thing she did was make herself familiar with the layout of this place where she would be working. Two more rooms opened off this one. The first proved to be George Howard's living quarters—his sleeping cot and his clothes hanging from nails on the wall. She quickly closed that door and tried the second, finding a small lab and storage facility. That was what she was looking for.

She set herself to checking supplies and equipment and opening cabinet doors to find out where everything was kept, pleased to see that the doctor's shelves were

60

well stocked and neatly labeled. She felt good to be busy again in her chosen surroundings. Her spirits were considerably raised after a good night's rest in Madge Devere's comfortable guest room and with that tiring stage journey behind her.

Only one nagging thought continued to trouble her: the thought of Frank Gannon and the way she had hurt and angered him last evening without any such intention. She would give almost anything not to have had that happen. Yet there seemed nothing she could do about it now, and she might as well accept the fact. It would be more fitting—she reminded herself with a pang almost of guilt—if she gave thought to the problem of finding her missing husband. After all, Jim Kirby was the one and only reason for her being here in the Washoe.

She had just returned to the consulting room when she heard footsteps approaching the door. Opening it, she didn't know whether she or Linus Fox was the more surprised as the sheriff and another man confronted her. "Why, hello!" she exclaimed. "Are you looking for Dr. Howard?"

Fox acknowledged her with a nod. "Sure enough never expected to see *you*!"

"I just started working here this morning. I'm afraid the doctor's already gone about his chores."

The lawman frowned at this, but then he said, "Maybe you could help us? After what Gannon's told me about the job you did yesterday on that wounded stage driver . . ."

"I'll be glad to do whatever I can. Do come in." She stepped back so they could enter. Only now, as the second man in the hall shuffled past, she caught a glint of steel and saw there were handcuffs on his wrists.

Laura shut the door. She asked, "What seems to be the trouble?"

"Show her," Linus Fox ordered.

The prisoner wordlessly held out his manacled hands and turned them palms upward. Laura's brow puckered at what she saw. She looked sharply into Kramer's face, but the man's muddy eyes and stolid features showed no hint of the pain she knew he had to be suffering. Turning to the sheriff she demanded, "What in the world happened?"

The lawman's face mirrored her own fury. "I saw a brutal prison guard work him over this morning—with the hot end of an iron bar." He described the scene in a few angry words, adding, "It was a guard named Riling's idea of discipline. But I have another name for it!"

"Wouldn't anyone at the prison do anything for these burns?" Laura asked incredulously.

"The warden claimed it wasn't necessary. More likely they just aren't equipped for dealing with hurt prisoners. It's not much of a place out there, from what I saw. Anyway," Fox added, "this is how they turned him over to me."

"Is this the man I heard you say you would be taking to California?" Laura asked. Fox nodded, and Laura turned to the cluttered desk for a pad and pencil. "I'll need his name to bill the prison for our treatment," she explained.

The sheriff shrugged. "The man's name is Kramer. But you go on and do what you can for him. I'll pay and take it out of expenses."

"Very well," Laura said, laying the pad aside. "Both of you have a seat, please. I'll be back in a moment." Turning to an inner door, she paused and gestured to the handcuffs on the prisoner's wrists. "I'll have to ask you to take those off. I really can't do anything for him like that."

Fox was clearly reluctant to remove the restraints, but when she returned a few minutes later with the materials she needed, the manacles had been removed. Laura helped the prisoner out of his coat and turned up the sleeves of his faded blue work shirt. There were also blisters from the heated iron on his wrists and on one forearm, where it had burned through the material of the prison clothing. But these wounds did not look too serious. His hands, though, were another matter. They were dirt encrusted, tough, and callused from his hard labor in the prison quarry. The palms and fingers had erupted into blisters wherever the hot iron had touched, even briefly.

Laura poured cold water into a tin basin and immersed Kramer's hand in it while she laid out the instruments she would need. "Does that help?" she asked after a few moments. Kramer nodded briefly. "Ice would be better, but I'm afraid there isn't any. I don't even have any tea leaves. But I found some ointment that I think will help."

Gently she took his huge hands from the water and examined them again. "I'll try not to hurt you any more than I can possibly help," she promised, speaking slowly and earnestly, not sure how much the man understood of what she was saying. "Those blisters will have to be opened and drained. The burns are fairly superficial, and they should heal in good time. But right now you'll have to hold still and let me work on you. Do I have your word?"

Kramer's muddy stare met hers with little understanding. He seemed about to speak, then nodded almost imperceptibly. "Good!" Laura said, with an encouraging smile, as she started to work.

Although the burns were not really deep or dangerous, she knew she must be hurting Kramer. She tried to be gentle, using the scissors as sparingly as possible on his damaged flesh. Through it all he sat passively, making no sound. Only an occasional tightening of a jaw muscle showed any evidence of his pain. Even so, before Laura finished treating Kramer, there were huge drops of sweat along his temples. When she finally tied the last bandage, she was relieved that the job was finished.

"It will take about two weeks to heal," she said, as

she helped him back into his coat. "But then you should
be as good as new."

Sheriff Fox got to his feet. "What's the charge?" he
asked. When she told him, he took a couple of silver
dollars from a black leather coin purse and laid them on
the desk, accepting the receipt she made out. As Laura
began to tidy up, the sheriff turned to his prisoner. "All
right, Kramer," he said, bringing the handcuffs from his
pocket, "on your feet. I only hope we haven't missed
the stage."

There was no hint at all in Kramer's face of trouble.
Suddenly Laura heard a muffled grunt and the sound of
a blow behind her. Even as she turned, the thud of a
falling body shook the small office. She stared in disbelief.
Linus Fox was sprawled on the floor, unconscious. Bart
Kramer stood over him, the lawman's own pistol grasped
in one bandaged hand. Somehow he had managed to
grab the gun from its holster and strike the sheriff on
the head with it.

Though Kramer still appeared as stolid and emo-
tionless as ever, Laura realized he must have moved
with surprising quickness to take the sheriff by surprise.
Laura felt a stab of guilt, remembering the sheriff's
reluctance at her instructions to remove the handcuffs.
Unwittingly she had been the cause of giving the prisoner his opportunity.

She dropped to her knees beside Sheriff Fox and
saw that he was breathing. But there was no chance to
learn more. Suddenly Kramer spoke for the first time
since entering the doctor's house. "Leave him alone!"

Laura raised her head. The revolver pointed straight
at her, and above it Kramer's muddy eyes held a dangerous light she had not seen before. It was concern for
Sheriff Fox that made her automatically exclaim, "You
might have killed him!"

"Wouldn't of been the first," Kramer said harshly.
"Now, you do like I tell you. Get up!"

Slowly Laura rose. She was frightened, but determined not to let him see it. She looked at the gun and

somehow managed to keep her voice steady as she demanded coldly, "Are you going to use that on me?"

"I ain't goin' back to be hanged!" Kramer declared. He turned briefly to look through the window into the street outside and appeared satisfied with what he saw. He waggled the gun barrel in the direction of the door. "You come," he told her.

"Can't I get my hat and coat?" Laura asked.

After a moment's hesitation Kramer nodded, and she turned to get them. The huge man stood waiting until Laura was ready and then motioned her ahead of him with the gun. He opened the door a crack, and after a final check on the empty street he took her arm and walked her to where the rented horse and rig stood waiting.

When Laura realized she was to be his hostage, she tried to pull free, crying, "I'm not going to get in that!"

But despite the pain in his bandaged hand, Kramer's grip on her arm was too strong. "You want me to have to hurt you?" he growled. She stopped struggling at the warning in his voice. He lifted her onto the seat and then hurried around and climbed in beside her, shoving the sheriff's captured gun behind his belt before he took the reins. As he slapped the leathers against the horse's rump, Laura wondered why no one was about in the early morning. Surely it was time for the town to be stirring.

At the corner her captor turned left, keeping the rig rolling at a steady pace. Laura studied his profile, trying to guess what thoughts lay behind Kramer's heavy features and the stolid set of his mouth and jaw. Though he seemed intent on what he was doing, she had little doubt that at any movement from her—any attempt to leap from the buggy and escape—he would be able to seize and haul her back. That thought, and the speed at which they were moving through the dusty morning streets, convinced her she must go along with him and wait for a better opportunity.

They rounded another corner and then turned to the right. Laura had just realized they were on the main road leading south when they passed the last buildings of town and began picking up speed. Fear touched her as she saw any chance of escape or rescue quickly vanishing. Kramer whipped the horse with the reins, and Laura stared at the ground blurring past, considering for a moment hurling herself from the vehicle.

Then, without warning, Kramer pulled on the reins, dragging the horse to a standstill.

Laura did not know that the side road they had just crossed led to the prison, a couple of miles away. But she saw a horseman riding toward them and she heard Kramer's angry cry, "*Riling!*" She remembered Sheriff Fox saying a guard named Riling had been responsible for Kramer's burns. So this was the man who had tortured him! As the buggy rocked to a halt Bart Kramer was already digging out the six-shooter he had taken from the sheriff. Hastily he took a shot at his enemy.

It was fired too quickly. It missed, but it caused the approaching rider—startled and not sure where the bullet had come from—to draw rein. There was no hesitation in Kramer. Suddenly heedless of anything but his hatred for the prison guard, he tumbled out of the rig and started for Riling at a heavy run, trying to get into better range for a second shot.

Seeing her chance, Laura slid across the seat and grabbed the reins Kramer had dropped. With trembling hands she struck the horse a stinging blow across the rump and yelled to spur him on. The animal leaped ahead and broke into a run just as a second gunshot sounded. Laura looked back to see what was happening. Bart Kramer stood spread-legged, the smoking gun extended in both hands. Riling's rearing mount tossed its head in fright, while its rider appeared to be spilling sideways out of the saddle.

Laura glanced back to her horse and flicked it

again with the reins. When she looked back to the scene of the shooting she could see that the guard did not appear to be hurt. Riling was on his feet but keeping low, running for his life through the tall sagebrush. If he wore a gun he apparently had forgotten about it in his panic. Bart Kramer fired a third shot, but again he missed.

At that moment, the door of a tavern that stood near the edge of town opened, and several men ran out to learn what the shooting was about. Kramer noticed the onlookers and all at once decided he was in an unhealthy place. He must get away from the newcomers, even if it meant letting Riling go unpunished. Kramer moved quickly to the prison guard's mount, a rangy bay, which had settled uneasily after throwing its rider. Clumsy as he looked, Kramer could move fast when he had to. A couple of steps brought him to where he could grab the horse's headstall and trap the reins. Before the animal could shy away Kramer was in the stirrups and lifting himself into the saddle.

As he jerked the bay around, two men from the tavern broke into a run and began shouting to head him off. Kramer kicked the bay into a run and shot at the pursuers, making them duck. He turned onto the road leading south from Carson City, chasing the speeding rig, as a thin chorus of yells went up behind him.

Suddenly Laura was uncertain whether to keep whipping the horse or to try to turn the buggy around, risking a spill. Bart Kramer was gaining on her quickly, flailing at the bay with his heels while holding on to his hat with one hand. Behind him the men from the tavern were already leaping onto their horses. They had no clear idea what was going on or whom they were chasing, but they saw a manhunt in the making, and on the frontier that was generally enough.

Laura heard the pound of hoofs nearing behind her. Surely, she told herself, now that Kramer had a mount and a clear road ahead he would have no further need of her. But her heart sank as the fugitive deliberately swerved in front of her to crowd the buggy horse and, catching its harness, pull it to a snorting halt.

He leaned from the saddle to tell her, "I want you with me."

"No!" Laura protested.

"They won't risk a shot if they know I got a woman," Kramer explained roughly. "And by God, ain't nobody puttin' no rope around *my* neck!"

As he reached for her, Laura tried to fight him off. One fist scraped his heavy jaw but bounced off harmlessly. An arm encircled her waist and, despite her struggles, he hauled her from the buggy and lifted her into place behind him. "You better hold on!" he warned as he kicked the bay, sending it running.

Laura had to grab at his coat to avoid being thrown off. A chill gust of the strengthening wind all but took her breath away, and she felt the first sting of icy moisture whip against her cheeks.

Riling's bay was a well-built animal, and it ran strongly under its double burden with very little urging from Kramer. The pursuers quickly dropped behind.

Kramer seemed to know exactly where he was going. Without warning he suddenly pulled into a little-used side road where a gully pointed directly into nearby foothills. The ground began to rise, and in a few minutes they entered high brush. Still they bore on, hardly varying their pace.

The rain began to fall harder as the morning sky darkened even more.

Kramer turned onto another trail, one scarcely visible to Laura. Almost at once they were surrounded by scrub timber. The steady pace was beginning to tell on the bay. Laura was starting to wonder how long the horse could continue when Kramer abruptly reined in under the shelter of a big pine tree. The man stepped down, still holding the reins, while he gave a long scrutiny to the ground they had just covered. Laura stayed where she was, clutching the saddle horn. Her long skirts were soaked and clung damply to her legs. She could hear no sound of pursuit, only the gusts of wind that whipped through the treetops and the whisper of the thin, cold rain. She pulled her coat closer about her and shivered.

Apparently satisfied, her captor said, "I think we lost 'em. They seen, quick enough, their nags couldn't catch up with this animal."

"Riling is the one that burned you, isn't he?" Laura asked.

"Yeah." Kramer's face closed in a bitter scowl. "He got away from me that time, damn him. But he ain't heard the last of me!"

"And meanwhile," Laura said coldly, "what happens to *me*?"

The question seemed to surprise Kramer. For the first time he realized the predicament he had placed her in. He looked up at her, and his heavy features became troubled. He drew a long breath and shook his head.

"Lady, I'm sorry as hell, gettin' you into this," he said earnestly. "Especially after—" He held up his hands, their once neat bandages soiled, ragged, and stained with fresh blood. "You treated me real good, almost like I was human—somethin' no woman ever done. Wasn't my idea to do you no hurt."

He wiped the back of one bandaged hand across his forehead in frustration. "I'd turn you loose right now, only I can't rightly set you afoot—not out here in this storm. But I know a place that ain't too far where we can get dry. You'll be all right there and once this lets up, I'll see about gettin' you back safe. That is, if you trust me," he added heavily.

Hesitating over her answer, Laura looked at him carefully. A very strange man, she thought. She did not doubt that he was guilty of both robbery and murder. Ordinarily she would have been terrified to find herself alone with such a man. And yet he plainly had some good human qualities, including gratitude for the consideration and gentleness that she had shown him.

She would have done the same for any injured person without even thinking about it. Laura knew that Bart Kramer respected her and would treat her accordingly. She nodded. "Yes. Of course I trust you."

He merely grunted. "Let's be goin'," he said. "Storm looks like it'll be a real gullywasher." He swung back into the saddle and pointed the bay forward, into the slanting rain.

It was never quite clear to Frank Gannon whether someone looking for Dr. Howard had found the sheriff lying unconscious on the floor of the doctor's office or whether Linus Fox had recovered on his own and started out in search of his escaped prisoner. Gannon had been surprised Fox and his prisoner had not been aboard the morning stage when it left on schedule. But making sure the special coach with a remarkably sober Hank Monk was ready for Ben Holladay and Merl Lunsford drove other thoughts from Gannon's head. When Gannon next thought about the sheriff, it was when he spotted the lawman in an excited clump of men gathered in the rain in front of the courthouse on Carson Street. Gannon hurried to find out what was going on.

What he heard appalled him. He seized Fox by an arm. "Damn it, what about Mrs. Kirby?" he demanded. "She was there in the office, you said—but what happened to her after that? Has anybody seen her?"

Someone Gannon did not know spoke before Fox could answer. "You must be talkin' about the woman I seen. She was in the buggy, and when this fellow Kramer took Riling's horse, he dragged her outta the buggy and hauled her up behind him. Looked like she was fightin' him, too."

Another man added, "After that there was no chance of stopping Kramer. I know that nag of mine wasn't any match for the one he was riding. And nobody was gonna risk shooting a woman. He still had her with him, the last we saw of them."

Gannon became even more alarmed. He recognized the noisiest member of the group as Harry Riling. Riling had lost his hat while running for his life, and the streaming rain plastered his hair to his narrow skull. He stood cursing the man who had tried to kill him and who had escaped on Riling's own bay horse—a valuable animal with which he had won races against anyone who dared to challenge him.

The others listened without much sympathy. Riling did not have many friends among the people who knew him. It was Linus Fox who impatiently interrupted the guard. "If something doesn't get started soon, this rain will wash out any kind of trail Kramer has left. Do I get a posse, or do I have to go after him alone?"

"Not so fast!" said Jay Bellwood, the sheriff of Ormsby County. A short, stocky man with an officious manner, he surveyed Fox with a steely stare. "There'll be a posse," he told the lawman from California. "But you're outside your bailiwick now, mister. You don't give the orders here!"

"The man we're after is my prisoner," Fox reminded Bellwood.

"He *was*, till you lost him." Bellwood turned to the growing crowd. "We've wasted enough time. Any that's going with me, get horses and guns and be back in ten minutes, ready to ride."

Before the men could go, Linus Fox spoke up. "Everyone bring grub with you. No telling how long we might be out there." Fox met Bellwood's angry look. "*Somebody* had to remind them!" he said pointedly.

Frank Gannon saw the other lawman's face darken and recognized the signs of professional jealousy with foreboding. He quickly cut in to say, "Whatever you do, don't go without me. I'll be back as soon as I can leave word with my clerk and get a horse." He headed for his office at a run. His concern for Laura Kirby was too sharp to let him worry about the routine of ordinary business. For the time being the concerns of the stage line would just have to wait. Leaving word with his clerk, he loaded his guns and strapped on his gun belt. Then he got his horse and joined the other men.

Chapter 7

For Laura, the day had turned into a seemingly endless time of clinging to her place behind her captor's saddle. The bay horse fought the hills and the sudden descents, following dim trails where its hoofs slipped on mud and on the ageless drift of pine needles. Rain pelted them mercilessly, and the erratic gusts of chilling wind seemed to cut her to the bone. There was nothing she could do but endure it all numbly and let Bart Kramer keep the animal moving on a course that she herself could not see.

At last a whiff of wood smoke drifted by on the sodden air, and Laura lifted her head at the promise of a fire and its warmth. They had ridden into a clearing, and the horse lagged to a halt before a log structure that might have been a trapper's cabin. It was swaybacked, its roof appearing almost ready to sink into the ground, but the door and windows seemed intact, and from a mud chimney smoke was buffeted by the erratic, rain-filled wind. At the side of the shack was a lean-to roof resting on poles, with three saddled horses under it, their tails turned to the weather. When Kramer saw the horses he gave a grunt of surprise and displeasure. Apparently he had not expected to find anyone at the cabin.

Suddenly the door opened, and a man carrying a rifle stepped out. He was villainous looking, with patchy blond whiskers and a puckered scar under one eye. He squinted at the newcomers in disbelief. "I'll be damned!" he exclaimed, his jaw sagging. "What the hell are you doin' here, Bart?" He turned his head and yelled into the cabin behind him. "Morg! You won't believe this! Come have a look!"

A second man, looking even more dangerous than the first, ducked through the low doorway.

"You?" he demanded of Kramer incredulously.

"Sure, Teale. It's me," Kramer said. "Who the hell does it look like?"

Morg Teale was balding and dark-bearded, with an appraising stare and a mouth that never smiled. He stood with arms akimbo, staring at the bay and its double burden and then toward the dark edge of the timber. His voice was heavy with suspicion as he said, "Is this a trick of some kind? You're supposed to be in the pen."

"I thought y'all would be happy to see me loose!" Bart Kramer retorted.

"We'll wait till we hear the rest of the story. Who's the woman?" Teale's stare rested on Laura for a moment and then returned to Kramer. "You better do some fast explaining."

A hard gust of wind struck, full of cold rain. The bay and the horses under the lean-to roof moved about uneasily, and a long shudder went through Laura as she tightened her grip on Kramer's waist to keep from being thrown. "Can't we at least get inside, to a fire? You can see we're both of us about soaked clear to the hide," Kramer said roughly.

Teale's stiffness did not alter, but after the briefest of hesitations he shrugged. "All right. Put your animal with the others and come on in."

At any other time Laura would have been extremely reluctant to enter the building in such company. But miserable as she was, she was glad to let Kramer help her down stiffly from the back of the horse and to be led inside the dark, musty cabin. Welcome warmth greeted her from a cheery fire crackling on a mud-and-stone hearth. There was even an aroma of brewing coffee that almost made it possible to ignore the other, considerably less pleasant smells.

The single room of the cabin was dark and sparsely furnished. The dirt floor had probably never been swept, its littering of trash only kicked out of the way. A double bunk had been built into one dim corner. Laura was not sure, but she thought she saw a motionless figure covered by a blanket in the lower bed.

Bart Kramer grunted with pleasure at the fire. Without ceremony he pulled Laura over to it. A word from Teale had sent the third man—Laura caught the name Doolin—to a window to keep an eye on the edge of the timber, obviously wary of further company. For a moment there were no more questions, and the two newcomers placed themselves before the fireplace and soaked up the warmth.

Laura wished mightily that she could take off her rain-soaked petticoat, but of course that was out of the question. Even so the warmth was more than welcome, though at its first touch long shudders went through her as her stiffened muscles began to thaw. Kramer added some sticks of pine to the blaze from a small pile beside the hearth, and as the flames leaped and sparks went circling up the chimney he pointed to a blackened coffeepot hanging from a crane. "Anything in that?" he asked Teale.

"Help yourself," the darkly bearded man snapped.

There were a pair of tin cups on the crude table. Laura tried not to think of the last time they had been washed. Mindful of Kramer's injured hands, she reached for the heavy pot. Even without all the hard riding and shooting he had done the last few hours, the man's hands would be painful, Laura knew. Using her skirt to hold the hot pot, she swung it off the crane and filled both cups as he held them for her. She drank the strong, bitter brew gratefully. It helped drive the chill from her.

Scrubbing the bandaged back of a hand across his

mouth, Kramer asked, "You got anything stronger than this?"

Laura was praying silently, *Please! Don't let them start drinking!* and was relieved when Morg Teale curtly shook his head.

"What about grub? I ain't eaten yet today," Kramer said.

"Somebody must of got into our supplies. What was left, we've pretty well cleaned out since we got here yesterday." Teale added pointedly, "We're still waiting to hear you tell how *you* come to be here."

The fires sizzled as Kramer flung the dregs from his cup into it. "I sure ain't got anybody else to thank for it! Sitting in that jail before the trial—even after they put me into them damn prison clothes and slammed the cell door on me—I thought sure I could count on my friends. But I neither seen or heard sign of any of you! You too busy gettin' guns and makin' trouble for the Yankees to help a friend?" he asked petulantly.

"Don't blame us!" Teale snapped back, his scowl ugly. "We'd of done something if we could. I know Reb Jackman thought up a half dozen different schemes. Nothing would work."

Kramer was not mollified. "Reb's supposed to be a smart leader. Why couldn't he come up with nothin'? I can tell you this. I had deals offered me—lots of 'em. All I'd of had to do was tell the law and the stage company what they're dyin' to know about the guns and stirrin' up trouble we been doin'. Nobody got a word out of me—but I ain't sayin' how much longer I could of stood it!" He raised his hands with the grimy and bloody bandages Laura had applied so carefully. "You ought to take a look at these! Just a sample of what was done to me in there. But I swear I'll be gettin' even for it, yet!"

Morg Teale shrugged. There was little sympathy in his voice as he said, "All right, so you had a rough time. It was your own dumb fault for getting yourself caught in the first place. But how the hell did you get sprung? Some sort of general breakout?"

"Nothing like that." Kramer shook his head. "Fact is, I had a little trouble, a while back, across the line in California. The bastards over there been wantin' to get their hands on me ever since. They must of heard I was in the Nevada pen, so they sent a sheriff over with papers to fetch me back. But the guy was too sure of himself. It wasn't no great trick to fool the sonofabitch and take his gun." Kramer gestured to the weapon in the waistband of his trousers.

Teale looked at Kramer skeptically. "His horse, too?" he asked.

"Well, that's sort of another story."

Doolin, listening from his post at the window, turned to the others. "The horse looked hard-ridden to me, Kramer. You real sure you ain't got a posse chasin' you?"

"D'you think I'm stupid?" the big man retorted, angry color surging through his heavy features. "Well, all right. Maybe there was a little trouble before I got clear of town. But they couldn't keep up with that bay. Once I got in the hills, I was careful not to leave no trail a posse could follow. Even if I had, the storm would of washed out the sign before now."

"That's what *you* say," Doolin muttered, clearly unconvinced. "We ain't gonna be happy about it if you've risked bringin' the law in here on top of us. And Reb Jackman'll be pretty pissed if you've ruined his plans!"

"How'd I even know there'd be anyone here?" Kramer protested, clearly puzzled by the attitude of the two men. "We never did use this shack much. Only reason I thought of it, we needed a place where the pair of us could get dry."

Teale suddenly turned and looked at Laura again. Something in his eye made her catch her breath and tighten her grip on the cup she was holding. "Maybe that's one thing at least we can thank you for," Teale told Kramer. "It's been quite a spell since anyone brought in a woman for us, let alone one that looked anything like as good as this one!"

Bart Kramer saw Laura's revulsion at the man's suggestion, and he scowled. "Now, hold on!" he shouted. "She ain't for you! She was just to keep anybody from usin' their guns on me. I've already promised her she gets back safe to Carson City. She just ain't the kind you figure."

"No?" Teale's bold stare raked Laura's body, his mouth twisted lasciviously. "Just what kind is she, then?"

"A lady, dammit! If you gotta know, she's a lady doctor. She fixed my hands up after that prison guard got through burnin' 'em. I owe her for that!"

Over at the window, Doolin was staring at Laura. "A doctor?" he echoed, incredulously. "A female? Well, hell—why didn't you say so before? Maybe she can do somethin' for Yancey." At Kramer's puzzled look Doolin gestured toward the corner bunk and the motionless shape that occupied it.

"What's the matter with him?" Kramer asked.

"Yancey took a bullet yesterday afternoon, the other side of Genoa, when we was trying to close in on a stage," Teale explained. "He was bad hit. Reb turned him over to the two of us to take care of. Since this was the closest place we knew, we fetched him here, but we ain't been able to do much for him." He nodded to Laura. "So let's see what you can do."

"Very well," she said coldly. She set her cup on the table and walked over to the bunk, aware all their eyes were following her every move. She drew back the filthy blanket and looked at the hurt man—apparently the one Linus Fox had shot.

Her teeth bit at her lower lip. The clothing had been cut away from Yancey's upper body, and for lack of anything better, a compress of folded rags had been laid over his wound. Removing the bloody rags, she could see the damage the bullet had done. It had drilled the man's ribs, smashing one of them. The dark blood still pumped feebly from the ugly hole. Under its whiskery stubble his face was gray, an all too obvious indicator he was dying. His breathing sounded shallow and rapid, and when Laura tried to find a pulse in the arteries of his throat it was almost too weak to be detected.

Kramer joined her as she straightened and stood looking helplessly at the hurt outlaw. "What do you think?" he demanded. "Pretty bad, huh?"

"The man is dying, " she told him bleakly. "He has a bullet in his lung."

"Don't seem to be bleedin' much," Kramer said dubiously.

"He's bleeding inside. Frankly I don't know how he could have held out as long as he has," Laura explained.

Kramer sneaked a quick look at the outlaws, watching them from across the room. He said in a low voice, "I don't much like the way them two are actin'. You sure there ain't nothin' at all you can do?"

"There's nothing anyone can do." Laura turned to the others and shook her head. "I'm sorry," she told them. "I wish there was hope for him, but I'm afraid there isn't."

Doolin scowled. "Maybe what it is, you figure it ain't worth dirtyin' your hands tryin' to save him!" he said harshly.

Laura merely looked at him, not deigning to answer. In the next moment Doolin got his answer—from the man on the bunk. Yancey's wasted body suddenly stiffened. There was a choking sound in his throat. Then, as blood leaked slowly from a corner of his mouth, his body went slack and his head fell loosely to the side. Kramer bent for a closer look, then straightened and announced, "He's gone."

Laura met their hostile stares. "I told you it was too late. Believe me—I'm sorry," she added because there was nothing else she could say.

With the faint, uneven rasp of the dying man's

breathing stilled, the cabin was suddenly very quiet. A burning stick in the fireplace snapped and settled. Teale and Doolin continued to stare at Laura, the direction of their thoughts almost visible on their faces. She forced herself to return their looks and tried not to show any sign of the fear that began to tighten like a knot inside her.

Bart Kramer shuffled his boots and cleared his throat nervously. "The gray horse, outside there under the lean-to—that was Yancey's, wasn't it?"

Doolin looked at Teale, who hesitated suspiciously before he nodded.

"Yancey sure won't be needin' him now." Kramer turned to Laura and said, "I seen they left him saddled. You go out and get on him, and ride away from here."

That brought a violent reaction from the other two men. "Nothing doing!" Teale exclaimed loudly.

All three men were armed, but the gun Kramer had taken from the sheriff was already in his bandaged hand. Caught by surprise, the others could only stare as he moved the muzzle back and forth between them. There was a sheen of nervous sweat on his brutish features, but there was resolution as well. "I promised her," he said roughly. "I didn't make her ride up here so you two could bother her!" Without taking his eyes from Teale and Doolin, he turned slightly to Laura and said, "I'm watchin' 'em lady. You go on!"

Laura hesitated for a moment, frozen by the danger of the situation. She could not guess what might happen if she moved—whether Kramer would actually shoot the two men if they attempted to stop her or if he could even hold his own against the others. She was not sure if there were actually any loads left in the weapon, after the confused firing that had taken place earlier in the day.

But Teale and Doolin had no way of knowing either, and they might not be in a hurry to find out—or to try Bart Kramer's unpredictable temper. Kramer had created a standoff. The least she could do was take advantage of it. Laura nodded her heartfelt thanks, then moved quickly toward the door on trembling legs. She stayed wide of the outlaws, careful not to come between them and Kramer's gun. She lifted the latch and slipped outside, letting the door bang behind her.

The rain was still falling. In no time at all her partially dried clothing would be soaked again, but that was the least of her concerns.

Beneath the lean-to roof the horses looked weary and miserable. They had been kept saddled for hours, with only a scattering of feed on the damp ground for them. The knot in the stiff leather of the gray animal's reins gave Laura trouble but she finally managed to work it loose. The stirrups were too long but the saddle girth looked tight enough. She backed Yancey's horse into the open. The gray tossed its head and rolled an eye at her. Laura spoke to it calmly, located the stirrup and horn, and hauled herself into the wet saddle, settling her bedraggled skirt about her.

As Bart Kramer had predicted, the strange horse gave her no trouble. A kick of her heel sent it forward. She pointed it toward the dripping trees, and as it took her over the clearing she found herself listening tensely for any sound in the cabin behind her—angrily shouting voices or the bark of a gun.

Nothing came. But the anxious racing of her pulse did not ease, even when the trees closed overhead and the clearing and the cabin were swallowed up behind her. She thought about Kramer's reference to guns and "makin' trouble for the Yankees." Could the gang possibly be the troublemakers who were stirring up the Indians and trying to cut California and Oregon from the rest of the Union? Rebel sympathizers were actively trying to seize the West for the Confederacy. Laura decided she must remember the name Reb Jackman, since he seemed to be the absent leader, and tell Frank Gannon everything she had overheard. She shook her auburn hair and urged her horse to go faster.

Unknown to Laura, a rider had pulled up at the

edge of the clearing just in time to see her disappear into the scrub timber. He sat scowling after her for several moments, his bony fingers digging at the straggle of gray whiskers on gaunt and rain-wet cheeks. "A woman!" he muttered aloud. He could not imagine why she would be by the gang's hideout. He looked at the cabin again, watched the feather of smoke whipping about the chimney, and counted the three horses tied under the lean-to roof. Reb Jackman never liked a situation he did not understand, and this one made no sense at all. He swore and kicked his mount forward.

The horse matched its rider—a tough sorrel gelding, with a hide scarred from spur and whip. Like its rider, it had traveled a lot of distance and had a good deal more left in it. As it carried Jackman toward the building the gang's leader became aware of angry voices from inside, a heated argument that prevented those inside from hearing anyone approach. His scowl deepened. He had taken great pains to train his men against the constant danger of an enemy taking them by surprise.

He stepped down before the door, dropped the reins, and pulled the revolver from under his raincoat. He waded through the soft mud to the door, placed a boot against it, and slammed it open. Instantly the voices stopped. The men in the cabin whirled toward the doorway and froze as they saw their chief glaring at them and at the gun in Kramer's hand.

"Kramer! Where the hell did you come from? Put that gun away!" Reb Jackman ordered as he stepped inside and heeled the door closed. His glance flicked over Morg Teale and Cad Doolin. "Well? Somebody had better get busy and tell me what this is all about— and don't leave out the woman I just saw leaving here."

Teale spoke up. "Only thing we know, Kramer has busted out of prison somehow or other. He won't admit it, but I got an idea there's a posse chasing him."

Jackman swore. "And the woman?"

"Seems like he grabbed her for a hostage. A lady doctor, he says. But if so, she didn't do Yancey no good." Teale indicated the motionless figure on the bunk. Jackman glanced at it indifferently. "So he died?"

As Teale nodded, Kramer spoke up in defense. "Wasn't her fault. He was almost dead when we got here. Like she said, from the look of that bullet hole I dunno how he'd lasted the night."

It scarcely seemed to matter. Jackman flapped a hand impatiently. "Get on with it! Where's the woman gone to?"

"I didn't like how them two was talkin' about her," Kramer said. "I had her take Yancey's horse and get out."

Jackman peered at him with mad gray eyes. "And supposing she runs into the posse and leads them right to us? We're wasting time standing here. Mount up and let's ride!"

Doolin held back. "What about Yancey?" he whined. "Shouldn't we bury him or somethin'?"

"You want to try digging a hole in that slop? With the law maybe on top of us any minute? Let the posse bury him." Jackman's hawkish features scowled even more than usual.

"I'll do it!" Kramer insisted.

All their eyes stared at him. "Yancey was a friend of mine," he told them defiantly. "You go on if you're scared. Now that I'm free, the posse ain't been born that could drag me back and stuff me in that cage again. But I ain't ridin' with you anymore, either."

There was a sudden stillness, except for the constant battering of rain on the roof. Jackman said, too quietly, "What are you talking about? You want to quit the gang?"

"He's sore at us, Reb," Teale explained. "He holds it against us that we never sprung him out."

"You can't blame us for that," the outlaw chief told Kramer angrily. "We studied on it—we honestly did. But there wasn't any way."

"The hell there wasn't! That prison's nothin' but an

old barn, full of holes like a sieve. You coulda pushed it over!" Kramer said.

"We could have got the gang blown to pieces, too. And that's a risk we don't take for anybody. You know that. We got a mission, and until it's done no one of us matters! We're key members in the Confederacy's bid to cut the Union in two. We could hold the fate of the whole war in our hands. *That's* what's important!" In his fanaticism Reb Jackman failed to see the skeptical and half-scornful looks that passed between Doolin and Teale. "I'm sorry," he told Kramer, "but that's how it is. Can you understand?"

Bart Kramer's heavy features had fallen back into their usual sullen lines, but he said, "I guess so. If you put it that way, Reb."

"So what happens now?" Morg Teale demanded harshly. "You ain't gonna let him quit us like he wants, Reb. He knows too damn much—all about our hideouts, where we keep the guns, and how we operate—not to mention some of the important people you got connections with. He could do himself a lot of good with that, if the law should happen to get its hands on him again— like they did once already."

Jackman nodded, his eyes narrowing thoughtfully. Kramer must have realized he was getting into dangerous waters. He backed away one step, then another, until his hip struck the table behind him. "I wouldn't do nothin' like that!" he protested, almost stammering. "I didn't do it before, did I?"

"You told us you come pretty close though," Teale reminded him coldly.

Growing frantic, Kramer appealed to his leader. "Please! I ain't gonna tell nothin'! All I want is to get the hell out of Nevada. I don't like nothin' that's been happenin' to me here!"

But Jackman slowly shook his head. "It ain't as simple as that, Bart. Like Teale says, you've become a problem—walking around carrying all that information in your head. You've been caught, of course, and so it ain't rightly safe to let you out of our sight. I just don't know what we're going to do with you."

"It's obvious, ain't it?" Morg Teale told him. "Why don't we do it and get it over with?"

Belatedly Bart Kramer remembered he had a gun behind his belt, and he started a fumbling move for it. His fingers were only able to brush the handle before Cad Doolin leaned across the table behind him and rammed the muzzle of his revolver into Kramer's back. The big man stiffened, but as the gun dug harder into his spine, he gave up. His shoulders drooped.

Doolin asked, "What do you say, Chief? Do we get rid of him now?"

The room waited for the answer.

"No," Jackman told him. But he snatched the weapon from Kramer's belt and stepped back. "This is no time to make that kind of decision. We've got to be moving. Take him out and put him on his horse."

Even then, Bart Kramer did not submit without a struggle. The table went over with a crash, and it took both Teale and Doolin to drag him out of the shack, still bellowing.

Chapter 8

Frank Gannon thought sourly that an expedition with a divided command had damn poor odds for accomplishing anything and that the posse after Bart Kramer was a perfect case in point. It consisted of eight horsemen, only three of whom had ponchos or raincoats. The rest could only turn up their collars and hunch their shoulders against the cold, rainy wind. Their initial enthusiasm had largely disappeared. After a few hours of fruitless searching they dragged ahead in single file, silent except for the continuing bickering of the two men in the lead.

The two sheriffs could not seem to agree on anything. Jay Bellwood nursed a jealous resentment of an outside lawman who had the temerity to invite himself on the manhunt. Gannon had known in advance that he could expect no cooperation between the two of them. The worsening downpour made everyone miserable and, more important, erased whatever sign there might have been to follow. The hunt was becoming more hopeless with every quarter hour that passed.

They rode blindly through sloping land with dripping trees, the storm's chill sinking into their bones. The only thing that kept the posse going was the reluctance of each member to be the first to admit defeat. Most stubborn of the lot was the local sheriff, who could not let himself admit he did not really know every stretch of his home territory. To Gannon, it was obvious that Jay Bellwood did not have the slightest idea what he was doing.

Linus Fox had come to the same conclusion. Bellwood led them around a rocky spur, where they were confronted with a choice of routes, up a climbing gully to their left, or through a shallow pass between two shouldering slabs of granite. After the briefest hesitation Bellwood started to swing in the second direction. Fox suddenly pulled rein. "Any particular reason for that?" he asked, his angry words carrying back to the last man in the line.

Sheriff Bellwood gave him a scowl. "What do you mean?"

"I mean, I see no sense riding in circles! Why can't you admit we aren't getting anywhere? For all I know we could even be lost."

Bellwood swelled with anger. "Damn you, I've had about enough of your attitude!" he shot back, his own voice rising. "You invited yourself along. All right! This search is being made on *my* terms, and if you don't like them—"

Gannon groaned to himself. It was only a growing concern for Laura Kirby that had held him to the manhunt for this long, even though he saw clearly that what they were doing was futile. There had always seemed a chance of a lucky break, of stumbling on a clue, a hoofprint that the storm had not erased. However, if the entire effort was going to fall apart in useless bickering and dissension . . . He lifted his reins, determined to pull out of line and announce that he had had enough and was turning back, when the man behind him exclaimed, "Hey! What was that? Up there—I think I seen something!"

At the head of the gully, mist drifted through the trees, obscuring their vision. At first Gannon could make out nothing. Then something moved against the dull background, and he saw a figure on a gray horse that took a few paces forward and then stopped, as though its rider was unsure about approaching nearer. All the posse suddenly was alerted, watching the figure above them. There was a whisper of metal against leather as someone slid a saddle gun from its scabbard.

Suddenly Gannon cried, "No!" He pulled his horse about and seized the rifle barrel, thrusting it aside. "Don't shoot!" The next instant he gave his horse a kick and sent it into the gully.

The other rider seemed to recognize Gannon also and with a sudden wave of an arm, sent the gray horse working its way down the gully to meet him. When Laura Kirby's voice called, "Mr. Gannon! Oh, thank God!" relief poured through him.

As they both drew rein he scanned her face anxiously for some sign of the ordeal she must have gone through. "Are you all right?" he demanded.

The smile Laura managed did more than anything to reassure him. "I'll be fine, now," she said. It might have been something in the intensity of his look that caused her to raise a hand to her auburn hair and try to push the damp tendrils up under her hat brim. "Mostly I've been frightened—and cold." She looked past him, at the other members of the posse who were already pushing toward them up the gully. "I was never so glad to see anybody in my life!" she exclaimed. "Except, I wasn't certain at first who you were—whether it was safe to let you see me. But then I recognized *you* and knew I didn't need to worry."

"You're safe," he assured her with a smile. "That's the reason we're here." The other riders joined them, their horses milling about. She already knew Linus Fox, and Gannon introduced Sheriff Bellwood. "This is Mrs. Kirby," he said. "She says she's all right."

Jay Bellwood touched the brim of his rain-soaked hat. "Delighted we were able to find you, ma'am."

"Looks to me she found *us*," Sheriff Fox commented dryly. To forestall more bickering, Gannon hastily asked Laura, "What happened with Kramer—after you worked on him in Doc Howard's office and he slugged the sheriff?"

"I hope he didn't hurt you too much," Laura said

anxiously to Linus Fox, who made a deprecatory gesture with one palm. "He wouldn't give me time to do
anything to help you. He forced me to go with him—as
a hostage, I suppose you'd call it, or as a shield if
anyone tried to use a gun to stop him. He apologized
for doing it. I guess he was pretty desperate. He was
grateful to me for treating his burns—which I'd have
done for anyone, of course," she added.

With a note of impatience Bellwood demanded,
"So where is he now? How did you manage to escape
from him?"

"Why, he let me go. And as a result, for all I know
he could be dead by now." She frowned at the memory
of events in the cabin. "There were two other men who
wanted to keep me, and he had to draw a gun to hold
them off so I could get away."

Linus Fox said gently, "Maybe we'd better take
time to hear the whole story."

While the horses stirred restlessly and the rain
pelted them Laura told everything, including Kramer's
reference to guns and making trouble for the Union.
The names she mentioned—Reb Jackman, Doolin,
Yancey, Teale—failed to strike a chord with Gannon,
and when he looked at the faces of the posse he could
see no recognition there, either. "Bart Kramer insisted
on letting me go, the way he'd promised. The others
didn't like it at all. When I rode away from the cabin, I
was listening for the shooting to start," she finished.

Gannon asked Sheriff Bellwood, "Do you know
this cabin she's talking about?"

The local lawman had to admit that he did not.
"Maybe you could find it again," he said to Laura.

"I—don't know. I might."

Gannon heard the briefest hesitation in her answer,
and he wondered if he could guess what made her
reluctant to agree. "It could be worth a try," he told
her. "And we might yet be able to get there in time to
prevent bloodshed."

That argument seemed to have its effect, and Laura

nodded in quick decision. It was all Sheriff Bellwood needed. He slapped a hand against his saddlehorn as he said loudly, "There's our answer. So what are we waiting for?"

The rain had slackened off to little more than a mist when Laura's directions brought the posse to the edge of the clearing and into sight of the swaybacked cabin. Gannon admired the way she had led them to it, unerringly and almost without hesitation, over territory that she had never seen before that day.

And he also admired her quiet strength, the way she had stood up through her recent experiences.

The posse drew rein to study the scene before them while their horses moved restlessly, with steam rising from their hides. To Gannon, the cabin and the clearing had an unmistakable feeling of abandonment. The door was closed. Nothing moved, no drift of woodsmoke rose above the mud chimney. Laura spoke in the stillness, "There were horses under that lean-to roof. Three of them, besides this one I took. I don't see them now."

Sheriff Bellwood stirred in his saddle and rubbed a palm across his cheeks. "Looks like we may be too late. All right!" He swung down, handed his reins to one of the others, and drew his gun from beneath his rubber raincoat. "The rest of you—stay put, and cover me while I have a look."

At once, Linus Fox also dismounted. "I'll go with you," he announced, and got an angry glare from the other lawman. "You take the door, I'll try the window."

Bellwood looked ready to give Fox another lecture about interfering, but must have thought better of it. Perhaps he decided it was only good sense to accept a backup. The rest of the party, remaining where they were, stepped down to stretch their weary muscles after hours of riding. As Gannon helped Laura from her saddle, he thought she swayed tiredly against him, but the nod and tired smile of thanks she gave him showed she still had reserves of strength.

Silently they watched the two lawmen approach the building.

The cabin had a window of sorts, merely a square opening without glass, covered by a hinged wooden shutter that stood partly ajar. Linus Fox approached it cautiously, gun in hand. Bellwood headed for the door. He waited there as Fox eased up beside the window opening, his shoulders flat against the rough log wall, evidently listening. Then, with the barrel of his pistol, Fox gave the shutter a push. It sprang open as he leaped back, out of the line of possible gunfire. None came. More boldly then, Fox moved to look into the interior.

At what he saw he gave a shout to Bellwood, who instantly put his stocky weight against the closed door and shouldered it open. He disappeared inside, and Fox hurried around to the doorway to follow him in. The posse exchanged looks.

"Nobody there?" Laura asked.

Gannon shook his head. "Doesn't look like it."

The remainder of the posse led their horses into the open. As they reached the cabin Fox and Bellwood emerged, their guns still in their hands but obviously unneeded. Sheriff Bellwood announced gruffly, "There's a dead man inside."

"Kramer?" Gannon asked.

Fox shook his head. "Nobody we ever saw before. He's lying in the bunk under a blanket, with a bullet in his chest. Must be the one Mrs. Kirby told us about."

"Let me see," Laura said and started forward.

Gannon caught her arm. "No need for you to do that."

The look she gave him was level and direct. "I watched him die," she pointed out calmly. "I can tell you at a glance if it's Yancey or not. Why shouldn't I look at him?"

"You're right," he conceded.

He went into the cabin beside her, the rest of the posse crowding in after them. The room looked just as she had described it, except that the fire had died to a few glimmering coals and the table lay on its side, amid the rubbish that covered the floor. Laura went directly to the bunk in the corner and looked at the face of the dead man.

"Is it Yancey?" Gannon asked.

She nodded, her face expressionless. As the posse stood staring at the body, someone muttered, "You'd think the least they could have done was bury him!"

"Likely they didn't figure there was time," Jay Bellwood suggested. "Once Mrs. Kirby was turned loose, they'd have wanted to get out fast, themselves. Bart Kramer surely knew there'd be a posse."

"What about Kramer?" another man suggested. "From what the lady told us, he could be dead by now. Those other two maybe killed him."

"He must have been alive when he left here—otherwise he'd be lying dead alongside the other one," Sheriff Fox pointed out. "They must have patched up their argument, and the three of them rode out together. One thing's sure, the longer we stand here talking about it, the farther they'll get!"

The warning galvanized Sheriff Bellwood. "Yes!" he grunted. "Shut the window and close this place up to keep the varmints out, and then let's mount up and find out which way they went."

As they were talking the sound of rain striking the roof suddenly increased, as though someone had started working a pump handle. Outside Gannon saw at once that the clouds, which had earlier seemed to be thinning out, were denser than ever. The rain came down before the wind almost as sheets of water.

Gannon helped Laura to mount again. In his own saddle, he spoke to Sheriff Bellwood above the noise of the storm. "We'll be leaving you here. I'm taking Mrs. Kirby back to town."

The sheriff scowled. "Hell, I thought you'd be

busting to lay hands on the crooks that's been robbing your company's stages!"

"I would," Gannon replied, "if I thought there was any chance of doing it. But this storm isn't going to let up. It's getting worse by the minute. Even if you pick up a trail it won't be for long."

"Anybody else?" Bellwood turned to glare around at the other members of the posse. "Any more of you that feels like quitting?"

They exchanged looks, but nobody answered. Gannon suspected more than one secretly wished he could turn back, but the lawman's bullying manner intimidated them. Finally Bellwood let his stare rest on the rival sheriff from the state of California in an open challenge. Linus Fox had been nodding agreement as Gannon spoke, but Bellwood's challenge put him in a tough position. Fox hesitated. Then, rather than reap the other sheriff's scorn by refusing to continue, Fox clamped his jaw and shrugged instead.

Triumphantly, Bellwood lifted the reins. "All right!" he said, pointedly ignoring Gannon. "Let's do it, then. Let's find their trail."

The posse rode away across the clearing, the shoes of their animals kicking up gouts of mud. When they had vanished into the dripping trees Gannon looked at Laura. "You ready?" he asked. She nodded, and side by side they turned their horses back toward town.

"I'd almost think that situation was funny if I didn't know otherwise," Gannon commented as they rode.

"Two sheriffs, you mean?"

He nodded and saw her smile slightly. "They don't seem to work very well together, do they?" Laura asked.

"Fox has got our local man so jealous of his rights, Bellwood's almost ready to commit murder himself! Between them and the weather, it's obvious they're going to make a complete botch of this manhunt. That's why I couldn't see the point in wasting any more time on it."

Laura's face became very serious. "I know what a

disappointment it is to have those men get away. Especially since you know they were among the ones that
tried to stop the stage yesterday and wounded your
driver."

She had put her finger on the one thing that vexed
him, a cause of deep chagrin. But Gannon only shrugged
and said, "Another time, maybe. At least you're safe,
which was our main reason for coming out—though I
don't think we can claim much credit there."

"But I'll always be grateful. To all of you," Laura
said sincerely.

For some time they rode in silence under the
weeping sky, working steadily downward out of the
hills toward the sage flats of the valley below. As they
paused to rest their horses, Laura finally asked a question that had been bothering her. "I've been wondering
about that man Kramer. Would you happen to know
what his trouble was in California?"

"Murder," Gannon answered bluntly. "According
to Sheriff Fox, a pretty bad one. Kramer robbed a
store, and in doing it he deliberately shot the owner
and another unarmed man. He was tried and convicted,
but somehow got away before the hanging. There's no
question that he's a violent and dangerous man, particularly when he's crossed."

"I see. . . ." Her voice sounded very small.

Gannon looked at Laura and saw her troubled
expression. He said suddenly, "Even so, you really
didn't want to lead the posse back to that cabin, did
you? Despite the fact he was the one who grabbed you
and hauled you there in the first place. I can see it
wouldn't be an easy decision—to set the law on him
after he'd risked his neck protecting you from that pair
of outlaws and forcing them to let you go. Well, anyway,
we didn't catch him, so now it doesn't have to be on
your conscience. For your sake, I'm glad."

Laura lifted her head and gave him a long look of
astonishment. "Why, thank you!" she exclaimed. "Thank
you for being able to understand that." She gnawed at

her lower lip and suddenly blurted, "It makes me feel more ashamed than ever, Mr. Gannon, about the way I treated you yesterday—as though I didn't trust you or want you knowing too much about me. I'm sorry."

He could not help but frown, remembering his hurt feelings of the night before. They urged their horses forward once again, riding in silence a moment before Gannon finally answered, carefully choosing his words. "It's nothing to be ashamed of, or for, Mrs. Kirby. I've thought about what Madge said, and of course she's right. We *were* strangers—and a woman alone just can't afford to take chances. But I do appreciate you saying this."

"We're not strangers now," Laura said earnestly. "I'd like to think we could be friends. At least, I wish you could stop calling me Mrs. Kirby."

Gannon smiled, his good humor restored. "All right, Laura," he agreed, nodding. "And my name is Frank."

The rain continued to drench them for most of their long ride, but by the time they approached Carson City thin afternoon sunshine had begun to peep through the clouds, raising wisps of steam from the roofs of the town's buildings. They rode directly to Madge Devere's house, where they found her on the porch, hugging herself against the chill of the day as she talked to Dr. Howard, who stood in the path below her, hat in hand. As Gannon and Laura rode up Madge gave a cry and came hurrying toward them. The doctor turned in puzzlement, then quickly followed.

Gannon dismounted and then helped Laura down as Madge tore through the gate and seized Laura, exclaiming her relief. They embraced like old friends, rather than like two people who had met just the evening before. Looking past them, Dr. Howard caught Gannon's eye and demanded, "Is she all right?"

Gannon nodded.

The doctor regarded him sternly for a moment, then muttered, "If you say so."

Madge released Laura from her embrace. "We've

been worried sick," she exclaimed, "ever since word got around about the kidnapping and the posse going out!"

Dr. Howard cleared his throat noisily. "Well, I'm glad it's over, but I can't help feeling it was all my fault—hiring you and putting you in charge of that office, all by yourself."

Laura turned to him anxiously. "I hope you're not going to tell me I've lost my job. Not the very first day!"

The older man frowned. Apparently that was exactly what he had in mind, but when he saw the disapproval in the other three faces he reconsidered. His blue eyes blinked behind the rimless spectacles, and he said gruffly, "Well—no, I suppose not. It was the sort of thing that would never happen again—especially if we take the right kind of precautions. You come back to work when you're sure you feel up to it."

"Tomorrow's soon enough to think about that," Madge said firmly, and took Laura by the arm. "Come inside. You must be starved!"

"I think what she mainly needs right now is dry clothes and a chance to get warm again," Frank Gannon said. "Meanwhile, I'll see to the animals, and then I have to be getting back to the stage office." He turned to Laura and said seriously, "I'm glad that things turned out this well."

She placed a hand on his arm. There was warmth in the look she gave him. "Thank you again—for all you've done." Then she followed Madge through the gate in the picket fence and up the pathway to the house.

Gannon turned to gather the reins of the horses. "I'll just come along with you," Dr. Howard said. "I want to hear the whole story. How did you get her away from that jailbird? Has he been captured? Killed? Don't keep me in the dark."

The two men walked up the street leading the

weary horses, Gannon talking and the doctor occasionally asking questions.

On Madge's porch, Laura held back for a moment as Madge opened the front door. The younger woman stood looking after Frank Gannon with a troubled expression on her face. Finally Madge asked, "Laura? Aren't you coming?"

Laura started as if suddenly awakened. "Of course," she said, following her friend into the house.

Chapter 9

As Frank Gannon had predicted, dry clothing and the pleasant warmth of the kitchen, together with the quick meal of fried eggs, bacon, and toast that Madge prepared for her, were enough to offset much of the effects of Laura's recent ordeal. Even so, as the two women sat eating and quietly talking, Laura's manner was subdued. Prodded by Madge's questions, Laura briefly told of the day's events. But it seemed an effort for her to talk, and Madge watched her with increasing interest.

Finally the younger woman fell silent, and the conversation lagged to a halt. Madge shook her head. "Will you please tell me what's wrong with you?" she asked bluntly.

Laura looked at her blankly. "I don't know what you mean."

"Oh, come on!" Madge made an impatient gesture. "There's only the two of us. I want to know if anything happened to you up there that—well, that you didn't feel like discussing in front of the men."

"No, no. Nothing—honest!" Laura exclaimed quickly.

"I'm relieved to hear it. But *something's* the matter," Madge persisted. "Maybe you'll feel better if you can talk about it."

"Oh, Madge!" Suddenly Laura put her hands over her face and began crying. "I'm so mixed up!" she sobbed.

At once the older woman was around the table, to draw a chair closer so she could put an arm around her friend's shoulders. She listened to Laura weeping for a moment, before asking gently, "Do you want to tell me more than this? Does it have something to do with Frank Gannon?"

Laura straightened and drew back, the tears shining on her cheeks. "What in the world could make you suppose—?" Then her face changed, and her glance wavered. "How could you guess?"

"Believe me," said Madge, patting Laura's arm, "it's never that hard to guess—not for another woman. I've seen the way you look at him. And maybe you don't realize it, but since he brought you home it's been all I can do to get you to talk about anything else."

Laura's eyes widened in alarm. "Do you think—*he* knows?"

"I couldn't say. Even a smart man can be pretty dense sometimes—as I've had occasion to learn the hard way!" Madge smiled cryptically. "So do you want to talk about this?"

"There's nothing to tell, really. Except that Frank Gannon seems to me a very good man—a fine man— and he has had an effect on me like no one else I ever met."

"I see. Does that include your husband?" the older woman asked gently.

Laura's mouth twisted in pain. "Madge, please. You're making me feel worse than I already do."

"I'm sorry," Madge said quickly. "I've known women who wouldn't even bat an eye over this, but I also know you're not one of them. You're a person who'd rather let it tear you apart."

"I just don't understand myself!" Laura cried helplessly, shaking her head. "Or—maybe I do! I try to think of Jim Kirby, and I'm afraid all I can see is the contrast between him and Frank."

"Not to your husband's advantage, I take it. Do you love him at all?"

"Once I did," Laura insisted. "He was very handsome and full of dreams for the future. And he laughed a lot. Here's a picture of him." Laura smiled at the memories as she reached into the reticule on her lap and produced a small daguerreotype, photograph, which she handed to Madge. "He was always fun to be with—until it became clear that none of those dreams were ever likely to come true. When he became discouraged, things weren't fun anymore. He turned bitter. It was only then I saw that he was really rather—weak." The young woman sighed, and her blue eyes stared, unseeing, at the table.

"When he finally made up his mind that all hope for the future lay here in Nevada, for his sake I tried to believe as he did," she continued after a moment. "After he left I kept trying to believe, as the weeks passed and became months. Then the time came when I stopped even hearing from him."

Handing back the photograph, Madge suggested carefully, "Had it occurred to you, if that's the sort he was, that he might have just thrown the whole thing over as a bad deal? Decided to make a break—taken off for the horizon without saying anything?"

Laura shook her head firmly. "He wouldn't do that. Oh, no, not Jim Kirby! First, there'd have been a long letter telling how hard he'd tried, and how nothing had come right, and it was all the fault of his bad luck. He'd blame every other thing under the sun, except himself. He'd have told me to forget him," she continued, bitterly. "That, for my sake, he was going on—getting out of my life. I kept waiting for that letter, but instead, there was nothing—no more word from him at all. That's when I knew something must have happened to him. But I had to find out for certain, if I could."

"Do you think you ever will?" the older woman asked quietly.

"I don't know," Laura admitted. "Back in Sacramento it seemed reasonable enough. Now that I'm here and actually see how big a job I've set myself, I'm just not sure at all."

A burning stick broke and shifted in the firebox of

the stove. Madge asked slowly, "And meanwhile, what becomes of you and Frank Gannon?"

"Why, probably nothing. I hardly think he's aware that I'm alive."

"No?" Madge gave her friend an arch look. "I notice he took off for the hills quick enough when he learned what had happened to you," she pointed out dryly.

"Frank is simply the sort of person who would do that sort of thing—it wouldn't matter who the woman was. That's the truth—you know it is!" Laura insisted.

"Maybe." Madge spoke like someone who was suddenly distracted by thoughts of her own. She rose and crossed the kitchen to a window and looked out at an afternoon of mottled shadow and sunshine as the clouds finally broke and scattered. She did not appear to be seeing what was before her. At last she sighed and turned, her expression bleak.

"They always say misery loves company," she told Laura, a note of irony in her voice. "Would it make you feel any better to know you're not alone? That you aren't the only person in the world who isn't able to get over a man she can't have?"

Laura looked at her friend for a long minute, then said, "Do you mean Dr. Howard?"

The other woman grimaced. "So it's as obvious as that?" She looked unseeingly out the window again before continuing. "When Tom died I thought I would never meet another man half as kind and considerate as my husband. And I was wrong. Because there he was all the time! George Howard couldn't work a miracle and save my husband from the fever, but he got me through the worst crisis of my life. Afterward he always seemed to be on hand for me to lean on, to help me in every possible way. It just seemed natural, after a while, having him around. It was only gradually that I came to understand I'd fallen in love with him. For all the good it does me!" she added bitterly.

"He seems to think a lot of you," Laura protested.

"Certainly. Oh, we're the best of friends—but for me that's not enough! I want him to think of me as a woman. Instead . . . Well, the way things stand between us now, I don't know how much longer I can bear it." Madge returned to the table and sat down opposite Laura. "The banker here in town would like to buy my house. He stands ready to pay cash on the line any time I agree to sell. I ask myself sometimes why I haven't already done the only sensible thing. Why I don't take his offer and his money and just get out of this town and this part of the country before my feelings about George tear me apart!"

Laura shook her head. Tears of sympathy filled her eyes as she exclaimed, "I'm so sorry!"

Madge thanked her with a half smile. "No reason you should be. I only wanted you to see we're both in the same boat. Move over and make room!"

Frank Gannon's clerk was an efficient worker who kept the Carson City office of the Overland stage running smoothly during his boss's frequent absences in the field. Still, there were decisions, details, and reports of the line's operation that inevitably piled up, waiting for Gannon's attention. When Gannon finally reached his office he stayed at his desk long after hours, plodding through a mountain of papers. He was still going over reports when George Howard stopped in for a moment. Leaning in the doorway, the doctor regarded his friend with a shake of the head.

"I swear," he commented, "it just doesn't look natural to see you stuck behind a desk."

Gannon gave him a rueful glance. "It goes with the job. Always something to think about." He initialed a letter he had been reading and laid it aside. "Right now, for instance, with Barney Powers laid up in Genoa and Hank Monk off on special assignment with Ben Holladay, I'm short a couple of drivers. That takes figuring, to make sure I can keep a full schedule with the men I have on hand." He shook his head. "I almost wish I was back handling the reins myself."

Howard's amused expression showed that he did not really believe his friend. "Maybe, if you beg hard enough, Holladay will demote you," he suggested dryly.

"I've thought of that," Gannon said, half seriously. "Still, the job has its challenges. Ben thought I could handle it, and I sure as hell don't want to let him down. So, Doc, what can I do for you?"

"I just dropped by to see if you'd had any news from the posse. Nobody I've spoken to seems to know anything."

"Me, either," Gannon admitted. "But that posse was carrying saddle rations, enough to last them for a day or so. And they've got a couple of stubborn gents leading them, both too jealous of the other to want to be the one to call quits. *I'd* still be out there if I thought they had any chance at all. God knows, nobody's got any bigger stake in seeing an end to the gang that's been hitting our stages than I do! But between that storm and bickering among themselves, I can't believe they're going to get anywhere."

"Too bad." George Howard cast a glance over his shoulder at the night sky. "All the stars are out now. Maybe we're in for decent weather for a change."

"I wouldn't mind that in the least." Gannon stretched his tired muscles, the chair creaking under his solid weight. "I've got to make a quick run up to Virginia City tomorrow."

Dr. Howard looked at him with sudden interest. "I don't suppose you'd take Madge along? She's due to make a delivery to one of the shops on C Street. Managing all those hats and boxes on the stage doesn't work out too well."

"It would be all right with me," Gannon replied. "She can fill up the whole back seat of the rig if she wants; the horses won't mind. If you see her, tell her I'll have to be leaving early, though. That's a three-hour trip, and I want to be back in Carson City by nightfall."

"No problem there, I'm sure. I'll tell her." George Howard hesitated before he continued. "Not that it's my intention loading you down with extra passengers, but it occurs to me Mrs. Kirby might like to go along, just for the outing. I doubt at my age I'd have been up to it, not after what she went through today. But Laura Kirby's young and healthy. At her time of life they bounce back pretty fast. And if she's here to look for that husband of hers, Virginia City would seem as good a place as any to start asking questions. At least until I can find time for the trip I promised her to Aurora."

At something he had said—Dr. Howard wondered suddenly if it might have been the mention of Laura's husband—Frank Gannon's face stiffened. But the look disappeared and he said rather indifferently, "I guess it's all right. If she wants to come along."

Set back by Gannon's odd reaction, Dr. Howard hesitated. "You're sure? When I see her, shall I suggest it?"

Gannon took another paper from the pile in front of him. "I don't care. Go ahead," he said briefly.

George Howard studied him an instant longer before nodding. "I will, then. I'll ask her." He said good night and, still uncertain if he had done the right thing, left the younger man to his work.

Dr. Howard had been right about the weather. Dawn came clear and sparkling with the promise of a belated spring. Perhaps it was due to the weather, as well as to her good health and natural resiliency, that Laura Kirby seemed none the worse for the previous day's ordeal. She was eager for her first look at the famous silver camps of the Comstock Lode, and she was grateful for Frank's offer to see what he could find out about Jim Kirby. As they left Carson City and followed the stage road north and east along the Carson River, she looked about with interest at the flat stretch of valley lands through which they passed.

With Madge Devere surrounded by a mountain of

hat boxes in the rear of the two-seater, Laura had no choice but to take her place beside Frank Gannon on the driver's seat. She chatted pleasantly, wanting to know more about the history of the place they were to visit. He answered her questions, telling her what he had heard about the big silver strike of 1859 and about some of the characters who had played roles in its stirring drama: men who had been prospecting Gold Canyon for years, living on booze and beans and dreams of wealth, taking out a little gold and cursing the "blue stuff" that clogged their rockers—until someone thought to have it assayed and found it to be some of the richest silver ore ever unearthed. He spoke of Henry Comstock, who had not even made the original discovery but had somehow lent his name to the entire body of solid silver lying at the heart of Sun Mountain. And he mentioned "Old Virginny" Finney, who, having fallen down drunk and smashed his whiskey bottle, had declared that spot to be christened "Virginia Town" in honor of his home state.

"I suppose those people are all very wealthy now," Laura said.

Gannon shook his head. "That's not how it works, I'm afraid. Prospectors as a class aren't big on practicality. They wear themselves out chasing a rainbow, but once they get hold of one they don't know what to do with it. After all, it takes organization and big money to develop a claim into a paying mine operation. These men usually sell out for next to nothing and end up as broke as they started. Old Virginny fell off a horse and broke his skull. I don't think anyone even knows what became of Comstock, except that when he left here he didn't have a penny."

"How very sad." Something in her tone made Gannon give her a sidelong glance. The pain in her expression was obvious, and he wondered if she was really wondering about her husband, who had vanished into the Washoe country so many months before.

Deciding it was better not to pursue the subject

any farther, he dropped it and they rode for a long time in silence, except for the spinning of the buggy wheels and the steady rhythm of the horses' hoofs in the hard-packed roadway.

After a while Gannon asked her for news of Sacramento, a town he had visited a few times on business for the Overland. The morning passed before they reached the mouth of Gold Canyon. Fifteen years before, adventurers en route to California had paused to rest their teams and wait for snow to leave the passes before making their final onslaught against the barrier of the High Sierra. For practice, some of them had broken out pans and shovels and had tried a little prospecting in the lower canyon. A few of them had found sizable nuggets but had hurried on, thinking of their find as no more than a promise of what must wait for them at the end of the trail. After the big silver strike, some of the adventurers realized they had passed up their one chance at unimaginable wealth.

The road turned up into the canyon and became increasingly steeper as it began to climb the flank of Sun Mountain itself. Above Silver City, elbowing portals of rock narrowed the roadway to a matter of yards at a place known as the Devil's Gate. Beyond, the pitch of the canyon grew steeper, the barren mountainside wilder, and the narrow road more tortuous and crowded with traffic. They had to make way for huge ore wagons headed down to the reduction mills along the Carson River. The swearing drivers fought the steep grade of the road and the weight of their massive loads that threatened to overtake their teams of mules or oxen.

Gannon and his passengers passed through Gold Hill, a secondary camp, with slag heaps and a jumble of mining works crowding the rugged slopes. They crossed the hump of the Divide, and the road straightened out, becoming C Street. Virginia City itself lay spread out before them, its streets winding in terraces up and down the barren side of Sun Mountain.

False-fronted wooden buildings, beginning to be

interspersed with more solid structures of brick or stone, stood anchored precariously to the steep slope. It looked as if the mountain could shrug and send the whole town sliding off toward the desert floor, far below. The streets teemed with traffic of every kind. The thousands of human beings, the roar of commerce, the pound of stamp mills, and the rumble of powder blasting at the rich ore in the depths of the mountain all lifted into the thin mountain air. Gannon, who was familiar with the scene, saw that Laura eyed it with mingled excitement and stunned amazement.

He drove directly to the fashionable shop that served Madge as a market for the hats she made, and helped the two women carry the boxes inside. "You'll be wanting some time for sightseeing," he said when they finished. "I'll meet you here an hour from now, if that's agreeable, and then we can see about finding a place to eat. All right?"

"That will be just fine," Madge said.

Gannon took his rig to a public livery, leaving it with instructions for the horses to be fed and ready to be harnessed again by two o'clock. His business with the manager of one of the Comstock mines, concerning an overcharge claim on a recent bullion shipment, was finished more quickly than Gannon had expected. With that settled satisfactorily, he proceeded on foot through the ceaseless hubbub and bustle to a brick building that housed the publication office of one of Virginia City's three daily newspapers, the *Territorial Enterprise*.

In the cluttered office he asked for Sam Clemens. The clerk pointed silently toward the floor under their feet. Gannon nodded and turned to the stairs leading to the press room below. Though it was the basement, the mountain was so steep that a loading dock at the rear of the room opened directly on the level of D Street.

The press room was the heart of the *Enterprise*, the place where the paper was written and set into type by nimble-fingered printers, and afterward committed to a clanking battery of flatbed presses. During a press run, it must seem to an unsuspecting visitor to be a place of yelling confusion and earsplitting mechanical din.

When Gannon entered the presses were idle. One of them seemed to be under repair. Someone was hammering on metal, and there was much shouting back and forth as the mysterious activity continued. At a pigeonholed desk in one of the corners of the cavelike room, the familiar figure of Sam Clemens sat bent over the pad of paper on which he was scribbling quickly, oblivious to all noise around him. He did not look up at Gannon's approach or even seem to be aware of him until the newcomer touched Clemens's arm. The writer's head jerked up, and he twisted about in his chair with such an obvious start that Gannon apologized.

"Sam, I'm sorry! Didn't mean to take you by surprise."

"That's all right." Clemens seemed embarrassed and tried to pass it off without quite succeeding. He was his usual untidy self, and there was a distinct smell of brandy about him. Running his fingers through his unruly red hair, he said gruffly, "I thought you were somebody from the *Daily Union*."

Gannon frowned. "You still having trouble with the *Union*? I thought that had all blown over!"

"Well, if so, it's blown back," Sam Clemens told him. "I seem to have challenged James Laird to a duel."

"A duel! *You?*" Gannon was incredulous.

"Pistols at thirty paces, and all the rest of it. Sounds very heroic, wouldn't you say?" the redheaded man asked.

"I don't know." Gannon admitted with real concern. "Are you any kind of a shot?"

"Not that I ever heard of. The big question is, how good a shot is Laird?"

"But—my God, Sam! This is serious. I thought this whole Laird thing was just a joke," Gannon said.

Clemens shrugged. "When his seconds come around to see me, I don't expect them to be laughing much!"

Gannon was beginning to realize that his friend was in deadly earnest and that under his pose of cool self-mockery he was really worried and perhaps frightened.

The ignominious feud had grown out of an exchange of editorials about the Sanitary Commission, which was a charitable organization dedicated to looking after the health and well-being of Civil War servicemen. In a spirit of patriotism and horseplay, a single sack of flour had been sold and resold at auction up and down the Washoe, for a total of $30,000 in donations to the Sanitary Fund. It was all well and good, until the rival Virginia City newspapers began accusing each other of lack of zeal in honoring their pledges to the Sanitary Fund. When James Laird's *Daily Union* finally branded Sam Clemens "a liar, a poltroon, and a puppy," frontier journalism had gone a step too far. Apparently, matters were headed for an actual shoot-out.

Though deeply concerned, Gannon could think of no good advice or help he could give his friend. He shook his head and said quickly, "Looks like you've got enough on your mind. I'd better go along and not bother you."

"No, no." Clemens waved him back. "You have a problem? Let's hear it."

"Well . . ." Reluctantly, Gannon told him. "A couple of names I wanted to ask you about. You've been in this country longer than me, and in a business where you're bound to hear a lot of things that most of us wouldn't."

"So try me," Clemens urged.

"First, would you happen to know, or know of, someone called Jackman—Reb Jackman?"

Thoughtfully, Sam Clemens repeated the name. He took up the pencil he had tossed aside and made some meaningless marks on the block of scratch paper in front of him. He said slowly, "I swear, *that's* one I haven't heard in almost two years."

"Then you do know him?"

"Not personally. It's just that when I first came out here, it was a name I kept hearing a lot. Jackman . . . He had a real first name but every one called him 'Reb'—and he earned it! He may have been from the deep South, though I think more likely from one of the border states. But old John C. Calhoun himself wasn't any hotter for secession. When the war started Jackman got together a bunch of the same mind as him, and they went roaring around the Washoe taking out their feelings on anybody that differed from them." Clemens looked up at Gannon. "Burned some places and shot and hung a number of Union people. It looked for a while as though Jackman was seriously out to set himself up as sort of a Confederate John Brown. Well, he was crazy enough for the part!"

"And what happened?" Gannon asked.

"I really have no idea, come to think of it. Jackman dropped out of sight, and I never heard any more about him. I suppose I just assumed somebody on the other side did him in." Clemens gave the other man a curious look. "Why do you want to know about Reb Jackman after all this time? Where would you have heard his name?"

Grimly, Gannon answered, "It begins to look as though he could be leading the trouble going on along the Overland, between here and California."

Sam Clemens stared. "You're fooling!"

In a few words, Gannon told him of Bart Kramer's escape and of Laura Kirby's kidnapping and what she had reported hearing and seeing during her encounter with the outlaws. "There can hardly be any doubt of it," he finished. "They spoke of a Reb Jackman as being the one they took their orders from."

Clemens played with the pencil a moment, frowning over this latest news. "So he turned outlaw! I'd hardly have expected that. I thought of him simply as a pure fanatic on the subject of Southern rights."

"He could be both, maybe." Gannon suggested.

"Seems I heard you were a Johnny Reb, yourself," the writer said speculatively.

"By birth," Gannon admitted. "But I never worked at it."

Clemens wagged his shaggy head. "Pretty much the same with me. Back home, around Hannibal, most folks were of a mind to secede, but the rest of Missouri wouldn't go along. Personally, far as I was concerned, the main effect of the war was that it closed the Mississippi just when I'd finished my apprenticeship and earned my license as a steamboat pilot. That had been my dream, and I was so sore at everybody and everything that I just up and left them to fight their damn war amongst themselves."

As he spoke of his beloved Mississippi River, a noticeable change came over Sam Clemens—a brooding look of sadness and longing settled upon him. But he shrugged aside whatever thoughts were troubling him and said brusquely, "So I'm afraid I've told you all I know about Reb Jackman. Anything else would be guesswork that you can do as well yourself. I think you said you had another name to ask me about?"

"Right," Gannon said. "I recollect you telling once that you worked a claim for a while down around Aurora. I was wondering if you might remember running across a prospector there who called himself Jim Kirby?"

"One prospector? In a whole mining camp?" Clemens gave him a sour look. "That's like asking me to pick out a certain bee from a swarm!"

"I've got a picture of him." Gannon took out a photograph that Laura Kirby had loaned him. Sam Clemens peered at the darkly handsome face, with its frown that might simply be due to posing for long minutes with his head clamped in a brace, but which could also reflect some deeper dissatisfaction.

"Nice looking fella. Friend of yours?"

"I never met him. I'm asking on behalf of a friend," Gannon answered. "I'm told he was at Aurora for several months, beginning sometime early last year."

"Well, that lets me out," Clemens said, handing back the bit of cardboard. "It would have been since my time. I left there back in August of sixty-two, when I took this job on the *Enterprise*."

Disappointed, Gannon returned the picture to his pocket. "It was worth a try. I guess you've told me everything you can, and I appreciate it. I don't have to tell you I hope this trouble with Laird blows over."

"Uh-huh." As his friend turned to leave, Clemens suddenly called him back. "One minute! It just occurs to me, there's a man here in town who knew that Aurora camp a lot better than I ever did. He was there before me, and he stayed longer—Johnny Burgess. He and I were swapping stories just the other day. He hit it big last summer—brought in a claim down there that proved out really good. It's an outside chance, but it could be he might know this man of yours."

"I'll look into it. Where do you think I might find him?" Gannon asked.

"He's not hard to find," Clemens said. "The poor sonofabitch is working pick and shovel on night shift at the Gould and Curry."

"But I thought you told me—"

"I told you he struck it big. He also lost it. Sold out his claim for a good price and then blew the whole thing on a binge that's still history down in the Aurora diggings. He told me he's been flopping in a rooming house on D Street. I'm not sure which one. He should be waking up at about this time, in case you want to look for him there."

"I'll try to have a word with him," Gannon said. "Many thanks. And good luck."

Clemens turned back to his work. Gannon stood looking at the writer for a moment. Behind Clemens's facade of casual cynicism Gannon suspected that Clemens was trying desperately to hide his worry over the upcoming duel. But there seemed nothing more Gannon could say or do, so he turned and left.

Chapter 10

There were a number of cheap rooming houses nearby offering dubious shelter to the poorest and most transient Virginia City citizens who could at least afford the price of a bed for a night. At the second place he inquired for Johnny Burgess, Gannon was lucky. He was directed along a dark hallway lined with doorless cubicles, each barely large enough to hold a bunk and mattress and perhaps a single wooden chair. As he walked down the corridor, an assortment of smells and sounds assaulted him—whiskey and stale sweat, the groans and rasping snores of sleeping men.

The number of the room he wanted was painted crudely on the lintel. Gannon looked at the man sprawled, fully dressed, on the lumpy bed with nothing but his arm for a pillow. Burgess was probably not particularly old, but he had left his youth in the pursuit of rainbows. The slack cheeks bore a sheen of gray whisker stubble, his shoulders were rounded, and his hands permanently curved to the shape of the tools of his labor. It seemed a shame to waken him, but Gannon shook Burgess gently by an arm, and after a moment his snoring stopped. He stirred, muttering in protest. Finally the faded eyes opened and peered, unseeingly at first, at the man who stood over him.

"You're Johnny Burgess?" Gannon asked, getting a grunt that seemed to be yes. "Sorry to bother you, but it's important I talk to you if I can. Sam Clemens said you might be able to help me."

Having come slowly awake, the man groaned and

113

pushed himself to a sitting position, dropping his sockless feet to the splintered floor. He rubbed a callused palm across his head and down over his face, pulling his mouth out of shape. He yawned prodigiously, showing a few broken teeth. "Who'd you say?" he grunted. "Clemens?" Light seemed to break through the fog of banished sleep. "Oh—you mean old Mark Twain!" More and more, people who knew Clemens personally were beginning to call him by his pen name, as his writing became more widely known and quoted. "Sure! Have a chair."

There was only one, a rickety object with its back missing. Gannon let himself onto it gingerly. Johnny Burgess leaned to grope under the bed and brought up a half-empty bottle of vile-looking whiskey. He shoved out the cork with a thumb and took a long drag, then offered the bottle to his visitor. When Gannon shook his head, Burgess had another pull at it himself. That seemed to finish cleaning out his head, for when he rammed the cork home again his eyes were clearer. "I guess I'm up now. So what did Mark think I could do for you?" he asked.

"He said you might tell me about a man I'm trying to locate, someone you might have run into down at Aurora. Maybe you could recognize him from his picture. I'm Frank Gannon," he added, as he took the photograph from his pocket. "The man I'm looking for goes by the name of Jim Kirby." Gannon thought for a moment the name might have struck a chord, but when he handed over the picture Burgess shook his head as he squinted at it.

"You don't know him, then?" Gannon asked.

"Nope. When you said Kirby it seemed for a minute—but that ain't the face. . . ." He shook his head, started to hand the photo back, then said, "Lemme see that again." As Gannon watched he studied the likeness a second time. He placed a grimy hand over the lower half of it and considered it carefully, his head on one side and mouth screwed up in concentration.

Suddenly he nodded. "Hell! It's the beard! That's right—the man I knew might have looked something like this, only by then he'd sprouted whiskers like the inside of a mattress. Most of the boys sort of forget their razors when they hit the Washoe."

Gannon felt a stirring of excitement. "You sound like this is someone you know."

"Jim Kirby, you said? Well, we didn't use last names much, but—yeah, the Jim part sounds right. Sure—I got him placed now," the man went on, with growing certainty. "I remember he sported a fancy ring on his left hand. Wore it all the time, except when he was doing heavy work on his claim. Told me it was a genuine ruby—his wife gave it to him." The grizzled head nodded vigorously. "No doubt about it, this is him, all right."

Burgess fell silent, contemplating the face in the picture. Gannon stirred impatiently. "So, what more can you tell me? Do you know where he'd be now?"

"Why, he's dead," Burgess said, as if surprised his guest did not know.

"Dead!" Gannon stared at him aghast.

"You sound like you think I'm lying! Mister, that Aurora is one tough camp. At least, it was last season when I was there. A shooting was nothing out of the ordinary. A man had to learn to look out for himself, or he could be killed for the mud in his sluice box!"

"I've heard as much," Gannon agreed. "It's just that it comes as a shock to hear it about Jim Kirby. You're sure you couldn't be mistaken? Did you see him killed?"

"I seen him afterward—I helped plant him. Oh, it was him, all right. Somebody had done him in and stripped him of anything they figured worth taking—including the ring."

"All right. I have to believe you," Gannon told him heavily. He drew a long breath, reluctant to think about a task that lay ahead. "You've been a lot of help."

He took the picture and slipped it into his pocket while getting to his feet. "I thank you."

"Sure." Burgess had already dismissed him and was reaching again for his bottle. He did not look up as Gannon left.

His business had taken longer than he had expected. When Gannon arrived at the International Hotel he found Laura and Madge already in the lobby, waiting for him and more than ready to eat. He apologized for the delay as he escorted them into the dining room. Though he had been steeling himself for the moment when he would have to tell Laura what he knew, Gannon decided that this was not the right time or place. Glad of the momentary reprieve and yet feeling guilty at what he suspected was really cowardice, he found himself with very little to say.

Fortunately Madge was in a mood for celebration, with a check in her purse that was a good deal larger than she had expected and an urgent request from the dealer for more of her work. The hats she created were finding a good reception and even better prices from the affluent ladies of the Comstock. And Laura had seen much that she wanted to talk about. She knew the booming cities of California, but they had not quite prepared her for Virginia City, with its liveliness and its raw desert setting, or for the elegance of the hotel, with its linen, silver, and crystal table service and one of the only two elevators west of the Missouri River. She exclaimed over the number of choices on the menu and the excellence of the food when it was finally brought to their table.

A time or two Gannon found Laura's blue eyes resting on him, as though she sensed something was wrong. He made an effort to throw off his mood and enter into the spirit of the occasion, but he continued to be troubled by the secret he harbored. After they finished eating he got the carriage, and they drove about the steep and teeming avenues of the city. He showed Laura the homes of the silver kings—Mackay, Sharon,

Hearst, and the other millionaires who had been created by Washoe silver. He pointed out the mines whose sheds and shafts—with chimneys belching smoke into the desert sky—stood cheek by jowl with the buildings of the town itself.

Soon it was time to leave, if they expected to cover the fifteen miles to Carson City before nightfall. The women had done some shopping, and their parcels were stowed away on the rear seat. With Laura again beside him and Madge in the back, Gannon sent his team over the rutted road. Virginia City quickly was left behind as they descended Gold Canyon to the Carson Valley far below.

Something of his own somber mood seemed to affect his companions, and during the hours of the return journey the silences grew longer and longer. They drew up before Madge's home in the fading sunset, and Gannon turned to the young woman at his side. Though he tried to lighten his words, they sounded ominous to his own ears as he said, "I'd like to talk with you for a minute."

Laura looked at him quickly. From her expression, she might almost have been waiting for his words. "Very well," she said calmly. "Come inside." Madge told them they could use the living room.

Moments later the two of them faced each other in the silence of the room. "Shall we sit down?" Laura indicated the horsehair sofa.

Gannon sat and took the photograph from his pocket. "I wanted to give this back to you," he said.

"Oh." As she accepted it her fingers touched his, and they felt cold. "I understand," she said. "I really didn't expect you'd find out anything. That would be too much to hope for, so soon."

Gannon drew a breath. "On the contrary. That part of it turned out a lot easier than anyone would have believed."

Suddenly Laura became very still. Her eyes searched

his face, and what she read there seemed to fill her with apprehension. "What are you telling me?"

"I happened to talk to the right people, and I was led straight to a man who knew your husband—at least he thinks he recognized the picture. Let me ask you one question. Would there be something you gave your husband that would help to identify him? I'm talking about a personal item, that anyone meeting him might be almost certain to notice and remember?"

Laura's eyes widened. Suddenly she was ahead of him. "You must mean—the *ring!*" When he did not speak she went on. "I forgot all about that! Actually it wasn't very expensive—not a real ruby at all, though he enjoyed telling people it was. But—" Her face drained of color. "Have I guessed what it is you're going to tell me?"

"I'm sorry. You just took away any real doubt. I'm afraid your husband is dead, Laura. Last year, at Aurora." As briefly as he could, Gannon told her what he had learned. As she listened her shoulders sagged as though they were receiving a terrible burden. Her mouth shook, and suddenly she turned away, dropping her face into her hands.

Gannon longed to comfort her. He put out a hand, awkwardly, but drew it back without touching her. All he could do was say, "I'm damned sorry. I'm even sorrier, having to be the one to tell you!"

"I know that," Laura said in a muffled voice. As quickly as she had burst into tears, she regained control of herself. She took a handkerchief from her pocket and dried her eyes and cheeks. When she spoke again her voice was leaden.

"Of course it's a shock, actually to hear this—finally! When Jim stopped writing, I knew in a way that something like this must have happened. That's when I really started giving him up. And I've had all these months to live with it and learn to accept it." She slowly filled her lungs with breath and straightened her shoulders. Turning to Gannon she said simply, "I do thank you for the trouble you've gone to, helping me to get the truth at last."

He waved her words aside. "One thing that's sure," he said gruffly. "You're not going to have any good memories of Washoe country to take away with you when you head back for Sacramento. It's a hard land, and you've seen nothing but violence in the short time you've been here. Now, on top of everything else—this!" He hesitated, unable to phrase the question he desperately wanted to ask. He took a breath and said instead, "Now you know your husband's dead, I guess you've got no reason to be staying in Carson City any longer."

After a single, searching look into his face, Laura turned away. She got to her feet in a way that told him there was nothing more for him to say or do. As he rose, hat in hand, she stood without looking at him, and there was a dead finality in her tone as she said, "I agree. There really doesn't seem to be anything now to hold me here."

It was almost an hour later when Madge Devere came in from the hallway. At the sight of her friend standing alone silhouetted motionlessly against the window, gazing out into the dusk, Madge exclaimed, "For goodness sake! What are you doing alone here in the dark? Where's Frank?"

Madge went to the table and lit the lamp. She settled the chimney and turned up the wick—and gasped as she saw Laura's face.

"My dear! What's wrong?" Madge asked, deeply concerned.

It was then that she noticed the photograph lying on the table where Laura had placed it. She picked it up and guessed the truth. "You've had bad news, haven't you?"

"Yes."

"I'm so sorry!" Madge told her, meaning it. It was her practical streak that made her continue, "Still, I suppose one has to be realistic. Though of course I know this must come as a shock."

"It's a good deal worse than that," Laura said in a dull tone. "I feel so sad for Jim! Perhaps he wasn't anything like the person I thought he was when we married, but he did the best he could. It just doesn't seem right that *nothing* ever worked out for him."

"Of course." Madge patted her hand. "You would feel that way—about anyone. But after all these months that have passed, you've got to start thinking about yourself, too. I think you know what I'm talking about, don't you? You and Frank," she added pointedly.

Laura turned her head away. "There's nothing between Frank Gannon and me."

"Are you asking me to believe that? After the day I just spent with the pair of you—watching you both, listening to you? I'm not exactly blind!"

"I think maybe I am," Laura confessed miserably. "I was beginning to think I saw things between us, but I know now they were never there. He just told me so."

"He didn't!"

Laura nodded her head. "In so many words! 'Now you know your husband is dead, you've got no reason to be staying in Carson City any longer.' He *said* that, Madge! Could he have made it any plainer that he isn't interested in me?"

"I don't know. I'd be inclined to say he was fishing, offering you the chance to tell him he was wrong," the older woman suggested.

"I know what I heard! And right after that he left—without speaking another syllable." Laura twisted a lock of her auburn hair miserably.

Slowly, Madge shook her head, stunned. "So you've been standing here in the dark—brooding over it."

Laura drew a deep breath. "I've been doing more than that, Madge. I've been facing facts. And I've decided he was right. There really isn't any reason now why I shouldn't be starting back to Sacramento—as soon as possible."

"You're upset," Madge told her, taking her arm.

"Come along. I've put some coffee on. No reason why we can't sit and talk about this sanely."

But at the kitchen table, with coffee steaming unnoticed in the cups Madge set out for them both, the silence lay heavily between the two women. Finally Madge asked, "When did you think you might be leaving?"

"On the morning stage, I suppose," Laura said sadly.

"That soon!"

"I don't see why not. It won't take me long to pack. And I've always believed that once you reach a decision, you should go ahead and act on it. Cut things off clean." Laura's voice became bitter.

There was a long pause before Madge finally spoke again. "Would you mind some company?" she asked in a low voice.

"You? Of course not." Laura frowned. "But—I didn't realize you were thinking about taking a trip."

"I'm not going on any visit," Madge said heavily. "What was it you just told me? 'Cut things off clean.' Well, that helps me make the decision I should have made months ago!"

The appalling truth dawned on Laura. "You're talking about Dr. Howard!"

"And don't tell me again what a good friend he's been to me. I'll never forget all his kindnesses," Madge insisted, "but I can't help it if I need something more, just as you do. And I've had plenty of time to learn that as far as I'm concerned, George Howard has nothing more to give. Why should I go on letting it torture me?"

"Even at the cost of giving up everything you have here in Carson City?" Laura protested. "Your home—and your business that's just starting to do so well. . . ."

"This house is too big for me and too full of memories. As for the business, I can take that to California with me. I'll get by."

"Oh, I don't doubt it a minute. In fact, I know

some people in Sacramento I could introduce you to. But—" Laura shook her head. "Are you really sure you want to do this? Sure enough to pull up roots, almost at a moment's notice?"

"Well, after all, it isn't as though I haven't been thinking about it. As for pulling up roots, there's not all that much I'll want to take with me. I think I told you that I know someone who has the cash ready to buy this place whenever I say the word—furniture and all, just the way it stands."

"How long will it take to arrange?" Laura asked.

Abruptly Madge rose from the table. "Long enough to put on my hat and coat and go sign the papers. And after that to put some clothes in a bag, collect a few personal things that can be crated and sent later, and, of course, to buy our tickets on the morning stage. Will that be quick enough?" She added earnestly, "This isn't a decision I ever wanted to make, but it had to come sooner or later. Now that I've made it I feel—" she stopped, surprised at herself—"*free!* As though I'd finally faced up to doing something I'd hoped all along wouldn't be necessary, though I knew I was hoping in vain."

"I know," Laura said slowly. "That's exactly how I feel, too."

The friends smiled at each other in understanding.

The spring darkness settled on Carson City. With no moon in the night sky the diamond glitter of stars rivaled the lamplight that marked out its grid of streets and buildings.

Approaching the town, Bart Kramer was equally aware of danger both in front of him and behind. Reb Jackman and the others undoubtedly would have discovered his escape from the hideout they had gone to after leaving the shack in the mountains. Kramer did not doubt that some of the boys were after him, determined to take him back or even to kill him rather than let him go. He drew rein once more to test the night again for sounds of pursuit. He heard nothing, but it failed to reassure him.

He let the horse stand for a moment, moving about restlessly under him, while he rubbed a fist across his heavy jaw and scowled at his dark thoughts. It was hell to be treated so badly by men he had ridden with, men he had protected with his silence during those months behind bars, bedeviled by a sadistic prison guard. As far as Bart Kramer was concerned, being disarmed and dumped into his saddle and taken to the hideout at gunpoint had spelled the end for him and the gang. Even so, he didn't really blame Reb Jackman. Jackman was still his chief—his leader—who, he was now persuaded, would surely have made the effort to take him from prison, except for the risk to the cause they all served.

But what about the others? Morg Teale, for one, had never made any bones over the fact that he had no use for Kramer, thinking him slow-witted and a drawback to the gang. After this there could be no trusting Teale or Cad Doolin or any of their friends.

The hell with them! Kramer swore to himself. He had managed to slip away from the hideout with both a horse and a gun, something they had probably thought he was not clever enough to do. He had no intention of letting either the law or his former colleagues interfere with his plans.

His hand tightened on the buttplates of the six-shooter behind his belt, and the dull ache in the blistered palm reminded him of a score he had to settle. After that, and only then, Bart Kramer would be able to put the Nevada Territory behind him for good.

His heavy features set with determination, Kramer kicked the bay horse and rode on toward the lights of Carson City.

Chapter 11

The supper Frank Gannon ordered did not interest him at all. He ate it doggedly, but the disappointing scene with Laura had left him with no appetite. The restaurant food seemed tasteless and stuck in his throat. All he had wanted was a single word of encouragement, the barest hint that he would not be out of line to think of competing with the memory of Jim Kirby. He knew he had handled things clumsily, not really knowing how to talk to a woman. But the answer he got was plain enough.

She was leaving. Well, no one could fault her for wanting to put distance between herself and the hard land that destroyed her husband. If she left now, of course, the chances were slim that Gannon would ever see her again. Yet she had given him no right to lift a hand or to say a word in an effort to make her stay.

At last he could not force another bite, and Gannon laid down his fork just as a shadow fell across the table. He glanced up to find Linus Fox standing beside his chair. Surprised he asked, "Were you here when I came in? I never noticed you."

"Looked like you were too sunk in your own affairs to notice anything," Fox replied.

Gannon ignored the implied question. "I've been up to Virginia City," he said. "When I got into town a while ago, somebody said the posse was back—without Kramer. You ran into tough luck, I guess."

"Luck?" Fox grimaced, and dropped heavily into the chair across the table from Gannon. "Stupidity would be a better word for it! That sheriff of yours doesn't know down from up—and the posse he threw together deserved him. If the storm had left any shred of decent sign, they'd have tramped it out good the way they were blundering around up there!" He shook his head in disgust. "I knew when you left you were showing sense. Only I couldn't give that sonofabitch Bellwood the satisfaction of seeing me call it quits!"

In spite of his own mood, Gannon grinned. The rivalry between the two sheriffs had exasperated him, but it had its comic aspect as well. "So who turned back first?" he asked blandly.

Fox shrugged. "It was sort of by mutual agreement— after a miserable night and still nothing to go on by daylight." He drummed the tablecloth with bony fingers, scowling over the unsuccessful manhunt.

"What will you do now?" Gannon asked.

"Nothing more I *can* do," Fox said impatiently. "I came here with extradition papers. I still have the papers, but no prisoner. The taxpayers back home aren't paying me to waste any more time on a wild goose chase." He shifted uneasily in the creaking chair. "So I'll be heading home, come morning. Meanwhile, have a drink with me, Gannon. You look like you could use one."

The younger man hesitated and then said gruffly, "Why not?" Gannon knew the sheriff's curiosity was piqued, but he was in no mood to explain to a casual acquaintance just what it was that was bothering him.

They had little to say to each other as they left the restaurant and moved through the lamplit darkness. They were nearing one of the town's larger and noisier saloons as Linus Fox brought out his cigar case and went through the ritual of offering Gannon a cigar and then selecting one for himself. They halted at a dark building corner so that Fox could turn a shoulder against the gusts of wind that scoured the street, scattering dust. As the sheriff dug out a match and prepared to snap it to life, a noisy trio of men approached and mounted the steps of the saloon. Fox glanced at them and gave a grunt of recognition. "Well! Look who we got here!" he muttered sourly.

The three men halted by the saloon door. The glow of an oil lantern clearly showed the figure of the prison guard, Harry Riling. Gannon had had few dealings with the man, but he had heard stories, all similar to the sheriff's account of seeing him go after Bart Kramer with a red-hot iron bar. Deliberate cruelty appeared to be second nature to Riling.

He seemed to be in high spirits, laughing boisterously over a joke he himself had finished telling. All three men were laughing as they started through the door. Riling let his friends enter first while he wheeled about and spit across the porch railing. Clearly visible in the light of the oil lamp, he lingered for a moment to peer along the dark street.

It was the last mistake he would ever make. He was just turning away when a pistol shot cracked loudly in the windy night. Riling was hit but did not fall. He seemed to stumble but somehow caught himself. He took another step toward the door, and the revolver spoke for a second time. It was as though the man's legs had been cut out from under him by the sweep of a scythe. As the echo of the two shots bounced off the building fronts along Carson Street, Riling fell. He hit the edge of the steps and then spilled down them limply.

Gannon had seen the second muzzle flash at the corner of the building on the other side of the street. Beside him Linus Fox exclaimed, "Kramer!"

"You think so?" Gannon asked.

"I'll bet a thousand dollars! You wearing a gun?" the lawman demanded.

"No."

Fox drew his own. In the next breath he was darting across the wide and empty street, trying to keep in the shadows as he headed for the row of darkened buildings on the other side. Whoever had fired the gun refrained from shooting again.

Judging from the limp, motionless shape of Harry Riling, Gannon knew the man had been killed. Riling lay as he had fallen, while the town began to stir in curiosity. Gannon heard voices shouting questions, doors being flung open, and the beginning of a trample of footsteps within the saloon.

Gannon was the first to reach the fallen prison guard. The way the body gave limply to his touch would have told him Riling was dead, even without seeing the slack features and the dark smear of blood. What he was really after was a wooden-handled, cap-and-ball Navy pistol he had spotted in the man's belt holster. Gannon had to jerk it free of Riling's loose weight. Ignoring the men who came pouring out onto the saloon porch, Gannon starting across the street to see if he could lend Linus Fox a hand.

The ambusher had probably fled. At least the sheriff had gained the corner where the shots had come from without drawing fire himself. Crouched there, Fox saw Gannon running toward him and swung an arm, gesturing. Gannon understood and veered aside, toward the far corner of the same building. He saw the lawman disappear just before he himself plunged into the dark slot between the houses, moving fast toward the rear and keeping the dead man's gun at the ready. If Fox had guessed right, by moving quickly they might have the ambusher in a trap.

The alleyway behind the building was dark, but with enough hint of illumination to show that it was empty. Gannon pulled up, futilely. There was nothing to do but to wait for the sheriff to appear, so they could compare notes and decide what to do next. Suddenly a commotion made him look to the left. A few yards away a man was frantically trying to mount a horse that did not want him.

A horse can sense panic in its rider, and this one was reacting strongly. It had been left tied by its reins to a fence post, and it was trying to circle away, constantly throwing the man off balance as he hopped on one foot, reaching for the stirrup and cursing. The man had his back turned, totally unaware anyone was near, until Gannon crept up and rammed the muzzle of Riling's Colt into the man's back. The man stiffened. His head jerked around, and his whole body went motionless.

His dimly visible shape had already identified him for Gannon. "All right, Kramer!" Gannon warned. "Forget the horse. Put those hands up—do it carefully!"

Bart Kramer tried to twist around for a look at his captor, but a prod of the gun barrel stopped the attempt. He trembled with fury as his arms slowly lifted to shoulder height, one hand still holding the gun that had killed Harry Riling. Gannon took the gun and shoved it behind his own belt.

Even then Gannon did not relax. He knew very well that Kramer was both dangerous and desperate. He said heavily, "Riling's dead. By your lights, after what he did, I can see you might have thought it was worth taking a chance to get him. But it doesn't look as if luck was with you."

Kramer swore at him. Gannon heard the sound of running through the alley and Linus Fox calling hoarsely. "Over here!" Gannon called, and moments later the sheriff joined them.

"Hey! Good work!" Fox exclaimed with approval. "And this time, we're gonna hold on to him!"

The sheriff took the handcuffs from his pocket. He jerked Kramer's arms behind his back and clamped the iron solidly to his wrists. The cold touch of the handcuffs took any remaining fight out of Kramer.

"No two ways about it!" the lawman told Gannon. "You stepping in is the only thing saved him for us. I guess you had a look at Riling. Was he dead?"

"As dead as he'll ever be," Gannon replied.

"I don't imagine anyone will spill any tears over him." The sheriff turned to Kramer. "I'd almost give you a medal, if I had one. But you still have a couple of murders to answer for in California—and on account of those, I mean to see you on the gallows." Fox paused for a moment. "There such a thing as a jail in this town?" he asked Gannon.

"Naturally. In the courthouse."

"That's on Carson, isn't it?" Fox asked.

"Just south of us a couple of blocks, and to your left," Gannon said.

"I only hope it's in better shape than that barn you people call a prison! I want to be able to pick up Kramer at stage time tomorrow morning."

"That's something for you to arrange with Sheriff Bellwood," Gannon told the lawman. "You go ahead. I'll fetch the horse."

Bart Kramer gave no resistance as Sheriff Fox prodded him toward Carson Street. Gannon grabbed the horse's loose reins and started after them. The horse was uneasy and did not want to go with him. The night wind had risen and it boomed along the dark alley in gusts that whipped up grit and caused the horse to balk and toss its head in an effort to jerk free. Gannon swore under his breath while the sheriff impatiently ordered his prisoner to wait.

It was at that moment that a trio of riders suddenly burst into view at the mouth of the alley some forty yards ahead.

There was an instant's surprise on both sides. The horsemen were no more than dimly silhouetted as they sharply pulled rein. But a few broken squares of lamplight behind drawn shades illuminated the alley, and it was enough to reveal Bart Kramer and his captors. At once one of the startled horsemen exclaimed, *"There he is!"* Another added hoarsely, "Hell! They got him!"

Sheriff Fox did not need a warning to know what would be coming next. He lunged aside into the shadows, hauling his prisoner after him. But Gannon was caught in the middle of the alley, plainly revealed in the muted lamplight. He had no chance to reach cover. Instead he let go of the reins and dropped to one knee, bringing

up the revolver he had in his hand as the frightened
horse galloped away.

In the confusion of figures at the end of the alley, a
handgun spurted flame. It was as though something
exploded in Gannon's skull. He felt himself toppling
into blackness and pain, apparently falling a great
distance. He was only half conscious of other gunshots
and the shouting of many voices and of the abrupt
ending of the fight as hoofbeats faded in fast retreat.
Frank Gannon sank into blackness, and all awareness
slipped from him completely.

Sheriff Fox had seen Gannon fall like a man who
had had the life shot out of him. The lawman swore,
but there was nothing he could do at the moment. Fox
had slammed his prisoner against the rough wall of a
shed and was crouched beside him in the darkness,
holding him there and trying to make himself invisible.
He lifted his own revolver and flung a shot into the
tangle of men and horses dimly silhouetted at the end
of the alley.

One of the horsemen gave a cry, not of pain but of
surprise by the near miss. At once there was the flash
and answering roar of guns. A bullet stamped into dry
wood somewhere above the lawman's head. It made
him wince, but he deliberately fired back twice. After
that Linus Fox moved quickly, retreating along the
shed wall, dragging Kramer by an arm as he sought a
new position.

Unable to see very much in the night, he set his
foot down on an empty whiskey bottle. It turned under
him and he fell backward, landing hard with Bart
Kramer's weight piling on top of him. Kramer was
struggling and panting. Fox could smell the fear from
his prisoner, fear that rendered Kramer helpless and
like so much dead weight. The lawman cursed and
flung Kramer off as more gunshots sounded, the bullets
coming nowhere close to him. Sprawled there, propped

on an elbow, Fox lifted his revolver and looked for a
target.

There was none. The horsemen had vanished, and
the entrance to the alley was clear. In the distance Fox
could hear a fading drum of hoofs that told him the
riders were fleeing rapidly. He also heard shouting men
approaching at a run from the direction of Carson Street.

Fox climbed to his feet and gave Bart Kramer a
hand up. Apparently neither of them had been hit by
any of the lead flying wildly in the narrow alleyway.
"Those were your friends, I suppose—trying to take
you away from us. The way they were throwing lead,
they didn't seem too particular whether they killed all
three of us in the process. Think about that!" he said
harshly.

The big man made no answer.

By now the men of Carson City were pouring into
the alley. They had guns and rifles, and one or two had
even brought lanterns to throw an eerie, bobbing glow
on the scene. When they saw Sheriff Fox and his prisoner they slowed and approached more cautiously, shouting questions.

Fox saw no point in telling the crowd anything,
since the attackers were already gone. He had other
concerns, and all he said was, "Stay back! I have a
prisoner here, under arrest."

Someone demanded harshly, "And who the hell
are you? You ain't Sheriff Bellwood. I never seen you
before."

Another voice answered. "It's the sheriff from
California. He went into the hills with us, after that
prisoner that escaped from— Hey! Is this him? Is this
Kramer?" The speaker peered at the glowering, shack-
led prisoner. "Don't tell us it was him that just killed
Harry Riling."

Fox was tired of questions. "Everybody back away,
dammit! Can't you see there's a man lying here, hurt—I
don't even know how bad, yet!"

That silenced the crowd. From a house whose back

gate opened on the alley, a man came hurrying, carrying a lighted lamp. He looked at the figure lying motionless on the ground and exclaimed, "My God! It's Frank Gannon—of the Overland! He's been shot through the head!"

"Maybe, maybe not," Fox said. "Where's Dr. Howard, or whatever his name is? Anybody know where to find him?"

"I'll try his office," someone volunteered and went hurrying off. The rest of the men stood uncertain and silent, all excitement gone. Sheriff Fox was depressed at the thought that Gannon might be dead. Though the two of them had been at cross purposes over the matter of Bart Kramer, Gannon had struck him as a good and dependable fellow. It was not a proper end for such a man—lying dead in a back alley, struck down by an outlaw's bullet.

The man with the lamp said sadly, "I don't like to see him just lying here! My house is handy. Somebody carry him inside, and I'll make a place for him."

Fox vetoed that quickly. "Not before the doctor has a look and says it's all right to move him. If he isn't dead now, it could be enough to kill him."

"I guess you're right," the man agreed. "I'll stay by him, then."

The sheriff nodded. "Thanks. You do that. I'll check back with you. Right now I've got a prisoner that needs disposing of."

The courthouse, at the corner of Carson Street and Musser, was a stone building that had originally been the Great Basin Hotel. It had been converted, with courtrooms taking up the second floor and with county offices and the jail on the first. When Fox marched his prisoner into the sheriff's office he found the jailer seated at the desk. He was a wispy old fellow named Millsap who was squinting at woodcuts of Civil War battles in a four-month-old copy of *Harper's Weekly*. He glanced up in irritation, apparently not able to see the intruders well enough to recognize them. "Well?" he snapped. "What is it?"

"An overnight customer for your jail," Fox explained.

"Who says so?" the old man retorted. "And who the hell are you?" He craned his head for a closer look. Linus Fox herded his prisoner closer, and as the sheriff's face swam into focus, the jailer scowled and grunted, "Oh! You again!"

"And I suppose you remember Bart Kramer." Fox cut off further questions by adding, "Don't get up. I'll put him away myself."

He had spotted the key ring that lay on the untidy desktop. Without waiting for permission he picked it up and steered his shuffling prisoner toward the door leading to the cells. He unlocked one of them and then had Kramer turn around so that Fox could use his own key to remove the handcuffs. He shoved the man inside the cell and slammed the metal door shut.

Kramer suddenly came alive. He whirled and seized the bars in his blistered hands. Glowering out at the sheriff, he complained bitterly, "This damn jail! It stinks even worse than I remember from the last time!"

Fox had to admit the filthy cell was in a condition he would never have tolerated in his own jail. But he merely shrugged and asked, "Whose fault is it you're in there? If you can stick it out, this time it'll only be for one night." He left the prisoner cursing and walked out into the office to find Sheriff Jay Bellwood in a heated discussion with his jailer. The local sheriff appeared flustered, uncertain whether or not to be pleased at the new development. "So! You brought our man in, did you? Congratulations," he said grudgingly.

"Thanks." Linus Fox tossed the key ring onto the desk where he had found it. "And thanks for the use of your jail. I'll be back in the morning to pick him up before stage time."

He was already starting for the door when Bellwood said sharply, "Now hold on a minute! I'm still in the dark as to what happened. I was eating supper when I got word that Harry Riling had just been murdered. As I was checking into that at the saloon, I heard gunshots, and afterward somebody told me you'd caught up with Bart Kramer and had been trading lead with him. And that's all I know."

Fox allowed a hint of cruelty to show in the smile he turned on the local lawman. "You did sort of miss the boat, didn't you? Too bad. Those of us who were around for it had an exciting evening—sure enough."

He saw the other sheriff's cheek muscles bulge over clenched jaws. Refusing to rise to the baiting, Jay Bellwood continued, "I'm also told that Frank Gannon is shot and likely killed. You realize, of course, that this changes everything."

"How do you mean?" Fox asked, suddenly wary.

"I'm talking about that extradition paper you got in your pocket," Bellwood said. "You can tear it up for all the good it's going to do you. I don't care who put his signature on it. Because now we got our own murder charge against Bart Kramer. Two of 'em, in fact. After this there's no way you can make Nevada turn him over to you."

Fox merely gave him a quizzical look. "What two murders would you be talking about?"

Bellwood snapped back, "Riling and Frank Gannon, of course."

"Aren't you a little confused? To begin with, Gannon isn't dead—or he wasn't the last I saw. And in the second place, Bart Kramer never shot him. Not with both hands shackled behind his back!"

"Who shot him, then?"

"There were three of them. It was dark in the alley, so I never got a real look. But I have to suppose it was some of Kramer's outlaw friends. Maybe Reb Jackman himself," Fox explained.

"Jackman!" Bellwood was startled.

"I'm only supposing. I wouldn't know any of that gang, even if I'd seen them clearly. Anyway, the shooting didn't last long, and they were gone before anyone could stop them."

"They wouldn't have if I'd been there!" Jay Bellwood said stoutly.

"But you weren't, were you?" Fox pointed out. "You were home eating supper. Maybe you'd like to call out another posse?" he suggested pleasantly. "That is, if you could get anyone to follow you into those hills that you've already showed you don't know anything about."

Bellwood's face turned beet red under the goading from the California sheriff. His fists clenched. He opened them and rubbed his palms along the seams of his pantlegs while he struggled to control his temper. "Don't keep changing the subject!" he snapped. "We're talking about what happens to Bart Kramer. So maybe Gannon isn't dead—but Harry Riling is! I won't need any more than that. I'm gonna talk to the judge and have that extradition paper set aside. We'll hang Kramer ourselves—in Nevada!"

"Oh? On what evidence? Where's your witnesses that saw him kill Riling?" Fox asked casually.

"Witnesses?" Caught offguard, Jay Bellwood stared. "But—somebody told me you chased him away from the scene of the shooting."

"They told you that?" Fox shook his head. "I couldn't swear who it was I chased. I certainly have no way of proving it was Kramer. I only saw a gun flash in the shadows and took off in pursuit. And if I have to talk to your judge, that's exactly what I'll tell him. Afterward, Frank Gannon and I simply happened onto Kramer and were returning him to custody when we got jumped." Fox shrugged helplessly and shook his head.

"No, Bellwood. Believe me—dark as it was on that street, you're not going to find a witness against Bart Kramer or anyone else. You've got no case . . . and California's conviction still stands. If you want him you'll have to wait until we're done with him."

Bellwood's steely eyes glared at Fox. The local

sheriff seemed to want to continue arguing, but Fox sensed that he already knew he was fighting for a lost cause. Suddenly beaten, Bellwood's face went slack, and his mouth settled into sullen lines.

"So I'll be back in the morning for my prisoner," Fox said pleasantly. "I expect to find him cleaned up and fed and ready to take the stage. I trust you'll see to it." Then he turned on his heel and stepped jauntily through the door.

Chapter 12

In a bay of rocks and trees, not far off the road south from Carson City, one of Reb Jackman's outlaw gang halted his mount and listened carefully. Morg Teale heard nothing more than the normal night sounds of wind stirring in black treetops and making a faint sound among the rock crevices. He steered his horse forward a few more cautious steps and again drew rein. Lifting his head he sent a low whistle into the darkness. Somewhere to his right came an answering whistle. Teale turned in that direction and repeated the signal. A pair of horsemen emerged out of the night and came to a halt beside him.

"I was beginning to wonder if you were coming. We've been waiting long enough to find out what's going on," Reb Jackman said sourly.

"I couldn't help it," Teale said. "The way things have been happening, I had to hang back and keep my eyes and ears open, so as to know what to tell you."

"All right," Jackman snapped impatiently. "Let's hear it. Did we get that sonofabitch Gannon?"

"I only know he was bad hit. How bad, I wasn't able to find out. Rumor has him dead, but no one seems to know for sure," Teale replied.

"And Kramer?"

"He's sitting in the county jail while they wrangle over who gets him. Talk in the saloon is that the local sheriff lost the argument, and Bart will be on his way to California on the morning stage, to be hanged."

Cad Doolin shifted in the saddle. "At least the

bastard got what he wanted. He got away from us!" he observed dryly.

Jackman shook his head. "Maybe. Maybe not. Kramer's still a danger to us, every minute the law has its hands on him. Something's going to have to happen to that stagecoach tomorrow."

"Tomorrow could be too late," Doolin insisted. "How can we be sure he ain't singin' his head off right now, gettin' even with us by tellin' the law everythin' he knows?"

The leader considered that for several moments, while their horses stirred under them uneasily. Finally he turned to Morg Teale. "Can you get a message in to him?"

"I can try."

"You'll have to do better than try! Somebody give me a light," he ordered. Doolin found his matches and struck one. The wavering light touched their faces as he held it, sheltered by a palm. Jackman dug a book and a stub of pencil from his pocket. The book was a much-thumbed Bible. He opened it to a blank end page and scribbled a few brief words before the match died. "Let's hope the bastard can read!" He ripped out the page and handed it to Teale with a warning. "Whatever you do, don't let anyone else see this."

Teale shoved the message into a pocket. "And afterwards?" he asked.

Jackman put the book away. "Cad and I have to get back to headquarters and make arrangements. You stay around town and keep tabs on things. Except for that lady doctor, there shouldn't be anyone in Carson that knows you by sight. When the stage rolls out come morning, I want you aboard it."

"I get you," Teale said. "I'll be there." He watched as the other two rode off into the darkness, quickly blending into the night. Then Teale spoke to his own horse and set out on the brief return journey to Carson City.

* * *

For the first hour after being locked in the courthouse jail, Bart Kramer had prowled his cell like a caged animal, from barren door to high, barred window and back again, as all the horror of his renewed imprisonment sunk in. Then he sat on the edge of the single bunk and had the shakes until he had to clutch the bunk's iron framework and force the pain from his blistered hands to steady him.

Kramer had thought all the damned lawmen would be harassing him, probing and questioning and jeering at him for his recapture. Instead, he had been left alone for some reason. Except for a streak of lamplight beyond the dark corridor outside his cell, he was in darkness. He listened to the muffled sounds that came through the walls and the narrow window above his head. Finally he stretched out on the hard bunk and lay staring hopelessly at the blackness of the ceiling, every muscle tensed.

Despite himself, Kramer had almost dozed off when something struck one of the bars of the window and dropped to the floor by the bunk. He lay without moving for a moment, not sure if he had dreamed it. Turning his head he dimly saw a tiny object on the floor. Grunting with surprise, Kramer levered himself off the bunk and reached for it.

It was a rock that had a piece of paper crudely wrapped about it with cotton string. He fumbled the string loose and spread the paper out on his knee. It was a blank page from a book. Turning it over, he saw something scribbled on it. He rose and went to the door of his cell to hold the paper up to the faint glimmer of lamplight. Finally he could make out the words: HANG TIGHT AND KEEP QUIET. YOU WILL BE TAKEN CARE OF.

That was all, and it wasn't signed, but he didn't have to be told that Reb Jackman had shaped those letters. He read the message again, slowly, his lips moving with the effort. A thrill of elation went through him. Obviously the gang had learned their lesson! This time, they knew better than to let the law have him. This time they had no choice. They had to get him free!

But by the time he returned to his bunk and sank down upon it, to stare about him at the dimly lit cell and the paler square of the high barred window, the first doubts were beginning to assail him. Could he ever really count on them again? Tonight, with that wild shooting in the alley—had they really been particular whether they rescued him or simply killed him in the process? Maybe all they'd cared about was shutting his mouth for good, one way if not another. What could he really expect from men like Morg Teale if and when they actually sprung him from the grips of the law?

Kramer shook his head, fists clamped until the nails dug painfully into blistered palms. Hell, anything was better than going back to California to hang! He must hold to that thought and trust Reb Jackman. Somewhere in Bart Kramer's soul was still some residue of faith in the man whose leadership he had blindly followed. Somehow—tomorrow, probably, on that stage road west of Carson City—Jackman would surely vindicate his faith and save him from his enemies.

Somehow Kramer had to believe in that.

It was almost two in the morning when Sam Clemens entered Carson City, his horse's hoofs making the only sounds he could hear as he rode through the sleeping streets. Even the saloons on Carson Street were quiet, and only an occasional burst of loud laughter or argument drifted across the stillness. The house where Clemens reined in was a two-storied, wooden structure at the corner of Spear and Division streets, with a corner porch and a bow window fronting the parlor. He swung down stiffly and anchored the reins to a hitching post. He seized a carpetbag in one hand and went up the path to the porch.

When he tried the door it was locked, so he used

the knocker. Getting no response, Clemens began to pound at the door with his fist and continued pounding until a glimmer of lamplight showed in the blackness beyond the glass. The glow came nearer, and finally the latch turned and the door was jerked open. His brother Orion stood tousleheaded and staring angrily out at him, wearing carpet slippers with his trousers pulled on hastily over his night shirt.

"You!" Orion said scornfully.

"I'm in trouble," Sam said.

"I take that for granted," Orion said wearily. "Only you never before got me out of bed at two in the morning!" He peered past the younger man into the silent street and at the horse standing droop-headed, looking as though it had been ridden hard. Scowling, he asked gruffly, "I hate to hear the answer, but is somebody after you?"

Sam hastened to reassure him. "No, no. It's nothing like that." Without waiting to be asked, he shoved his way into the house and walked to the parlor. Orion had been working until after midnight on the official documents that continually piled up in the absence of a governor, and a few coals still glowed warmly in the fireplace. Orion lit a second lamp, settled the flame, and put the shade in place. He looked again at his brother, who tossed aside his hat and unfastened his coat, standing before the fireplace and soaking up what heat still rose from it. "You want something to eat?" Orion asked.

"No." Sam shook his head. "But that was a cold ride down off the mountain. You got anything to help take off the chill?"

Silently, the older brother went to a cabinet and took out a bottle and a glass, which he poured half full of whiskey and handed over. Sam drained the glass entirely and placed it on the mantelpiece. "I have to leave," he said abruptly.

Orion's scowl deepened. "You just got here. Don't tell me you only woke me up to give you a drink!"

Sam shook his head impatiently. "What I mean is, I'm getting out of Virginia City—clear out of Nevada. I've got to!"

Orion stared for a moment, then sighed deeply. In a tone of resignation he said, "All right, let's hear it. What happened? It must be something really bad this time."

"It isn't anything new." Sam replied defensively. "The old trouble with Laird, of the *Daily Union*. You already know about that."

"Yes. One of your little *jokes* that got out of hand," he replied coldly.

"Well, it's come to a head. He's insisting on a duel!"

"So you really let it come to that! And now I gather that you haven't the nerve to face him." Orion ran his hand through his red hair in frustration.

"Hell, I learned too late that the fellow is a crack shot. And you know I couldn't hit a barn from the inside!" Sam saw his brother's disapproving stare and glanced away from it. "You can't expect a man to commit suicide over nothing," he protested. "Anyway, you can't have forgotten that dueling's against the law in Nevada."

"What of that? It happens."

"Only because the law is never enforced," Sam retorted. "But they'll make an exception in my case. Old Judge Turner will see to that! He's been sitting up there on his bench, just waiting for a chance to get back at me for those dumb pieces I wrote about him."

"Oh, yes, 'Professor Personal Pronoun.'" Despite the gravity of the situation Orion could barely suppress a smile. The articles *had* been very funny, catching exactly the stuffy egotism and pomposity of George Turner without actually naming him. But it had been indiscreet, to say the least, for Sam to go after the chief justice of the Nevada supreme court. Sam poured himself another drink and stared gloomily into the fire.

"Turner would like nothing better than to have me brought up before him and to stick me into that prison for the stiffest term he could manage. Well, I won't let him! I won't spend the summer cracking rocks or freeze my tail off next winter in that damned cellblock. Have you ever taken a good look at that place you got out there?" he demanded rather shrilly.

"I know all about it," Orion said. "It happens to be the best we can afford right now. Well, maybe you're right. Maybe this time you've backed yourself into a corner where you've got no choice but to cut and run for it. Where will you go? Home to Missouri?"

Sam stared at his brother in disbelief. "Are you fooling? There's a *war* on back there!" He shook his head. "Looks like it's California for me—and on the morning stage. There's only one thing." He hesitated and looked away, unable to meet his brother's eye. "Truth is, this means I'll be missing payday, and I'm caught a little short of funds."

"So now it comes out—now we know why you came to me!" Orion sighed and added heavily, "All right, give me a minute. Have another drink," he added as he started from the room, knowing Sam would help himself anyway.

The younger man was emptying the glass a third time as Orion returned with an envelope, which he handed over saying, "Here's two hundred. All I have in the house."

Sam glanced into the envelope, thumbed through the bills, and shoved the envelope in his pocket. "This is fine," he said. "Enough for the ticket and to eat on for a few days while I get my feet under me. I appreciate this."

"Don't mention it."

Orion looked doubtfully at his problem brother, who was a constant worry to him. Twenty-eight years old, he thought, and as irresponsible as a child. Not long before, Sam had gotten drunk and written a humorous article on the fancy-dress ball put on by all the prominent ladies of Carson City—including Orion's own wife, Molly—in support of the Sanitary Fund. Accidentally slipped into the columns of the *Enterprise*, Sam's remarks had accused the sponsors of diverting the money they raised for disreputable purposes. Naturally the ladies—and their husbands—were all up in arms against Sam and also against the harassed acting governor. Even Molly Clemens herself would scarcely speak to her husband.

"What do you plan to do in California?" Orion asked.

"You mean after heaving a sigh of relief? Damned if I know," Sam said, rather unconcerned. Now that he had the money and a few drinks under his belt, Sam was beginning to relax. He dropped into a chair and stretched his legs out in front of him, scowling at the toes of his boots.

"Surely you'd have no trouble getting on with any newspaper in Sacramento or San Francisco," Orion suggested.

"Newspapers!" Sam muttered disdainfully, and shrugged.

Orion pursued the thought. "There's nobody better qualified or more experienced." He hesitated. "If you'd only be willing to remember one thing."

His brother peered at him suspiciously from under his heavy brows. "And what's that?"

"Damn it, that a reporter is supposed to *report!*" Orion burst out in frustration. "His job is to state the facts—not embroider and exaggerate everything until it becomes a farce. I honestly don't know how you got away with it in Virginia City as long as you did—except that everyone on that paper is as crazy as you are!"

"Facts are a bore." Suddenly Sam sat up very straight, and there was a hard glitter in his eye. "You want to hear a fact? You want to know what my real trouble is? There's only one thing I ever wanted in this world—and I've lost it forever!"

Slowly, Orion nodded. "You mean, the river . . . Yes, I understand that. But Sam, someday this war will be over. Whichever side comes out on top, the old Mississippi will have to be reopened, all the way from Illinois to New Orleans. The boats will be running again—and you'll still have your pilot's license."

The younger Clemens doggedly shook his head. "You're wrong. That was a world that's ended. The war is changing everything, and nothing will ever be the same again. I won't be the same. Much as a body would like to, there's no way to go back. I have to go on—but to what? In a couple of years I'll be thirty. And what have I got to show for it?" Sam added bitterly.

"Well, you've written some things this past year that have made a lot of people laugh. Even the California editors have begun picking up anything they see in the *Enterprise* that has Mark Twain's name on it."

"Damn 'Mark Twain'!" Sam slapped a hand angrily against the arm of his chair. "You think I've got no more ambition than to spend the rest of my life as some sort of clown, standing on my head to make fools laugh? Never! A man needs more self-respect than *that*!" As suddenly as his outburst had begun, it ended, and he slumped back into the chair in despair. "I don't know. I just don't know," he muttered to himself.

Orion placed a sympathetic hand on Sam's shoulder but could think of nothing useful to say. "You're feeling low because of all that's been happening. Right now you need to get some rest," he said lamely. "And besides, if we're not careful we'll wake up Molly. Whose horse is that outside?"

"A friend's. I borrowed him," Sam said.

"I'll put him in the shed so he can be picked up later. Meanwhile you know where the guest room is. We'll get you up in plenty of time to catch the stage. With some sleep and a good breakfast under your belt, you'll find things looking better. Now come along."

Firmly but gently and with real affection for his younger brother, Orion got Sam to his feet and headed toward the stairs. "Good night," he said. Sam mumbled something as Orion went out into the night to see to the horse.

Frank Gannon awoke in a strange bed in an unfamiliar room, with morning light streaming in past the edges of a drawn shade. He felt totally confused and lacked both the strength and the will to move. A steady, throbbing ache filled his skull. When Gannon finally roused himself enough to touch his head, his fingers discovered a bandage. Puzzled, he fumbled at it.

He must have blacked out. The next thing he knew someone was standing beside his bed. Gannon heard the visitor breathing and felt a hand against his throat, apparently checking the pulse. He opened his eyes to see George Howard observing him gravely.

The doctor saw the puzzlement in Gannon's eyes. He nodded and said, "I know what you're going to say, so go ahead and say it. 'Where am I?' Is that what you want to ask?"

"I had thought of it," Gannon admitted, in a raspy voice.

"Anyone who gets himself hit on the head, those are his first words when he wakes up. It almost never fails. And next thing is to ask for water. Here, let me help you." The pain throbbed more sharply as the doctor put an arm around Gannon's shoulders and helped him sit up enough to drink.

Gannon discovered that he was fully dressed except for his boots, which someone had removed and placed under a chair a little distance from the bed. Dr. Howard smiled down at him as he settled back on the pillow. "This is where I had you brought last night after the shooting in the alley. If you look out the window, you'll see exactly where it happened. The man that lives here offered his bed, and I certainly didn't want you moved any more than absolutely necessary."

"Just what did happen?" Gannon wanted to know.

"You don't remember?"

"I'm—not sure," Gannon said slowly.

"Well, that can happen, too, in such cases—temporary amnesia," Dr. Howard said as he opened the windowshade for more light. Using thumb and forefinger to spread Gannon's eyelids, he proceeded to look at each eye. "Looking for sign of concussion," he explained. "But the pupils look all right. You were shot," he went on. "It missed by only a fraction of an inch giving you something a lot more permanent than the headache you're undoubtedly enjoying right now. But take care of yourself and you should be all right again."

The doctor rummaged in his black bag for his stethoscope. "That sheriff from California came around last night to find out how you were doing, and he gave me the details. It appears you had picked up that outlaw Bart Kramer and were starting off to jail with him when some riders suddenly showed up—three of them, Fox said. They tried to kill you. You don't remember this?"

"It's beginning to come back," Gannon admitted, one hand gingerly testing the bandage. "Fox and Kramer weren't hurt?"

"No, apparently the attackers were driven off. Kramer went to a cell at the courthouse, and Fox made arrangements to take him away on this morning's stage." Dr. Howard glanced at his pocket watch. "That would have been a little over an hour ago. I stopped by the station on the way over here, and your clerk said that the coach left on schedule and that the two of them were aboard. So by now they're well on their way to California."

"Let's hope so!" Despite a protest from the doctor, Gannon swung his legs off the bed. His head throbbed unmercifully, but he felt stronger than he had a few minutes before. "I don't like this, Doc! I'm certain it was some of Reb Jackman's gang that tried to take

Kramer away from us, and I think they'll try again. There aren't any stage guards to spare, but if I'd been on hand this morning I'd have ridden that coach myself. I'm very much afraid the people aboard may be in for trouble!"

Gannon was both surprised and alarmed to see the color suddenly drain from his friend's face. George Howard opened his mouth to speak but no words came out. "What is it?" Gannon demanded sharply. "What's the matter?"

"It's this. I found it a while ago," the older man stammered. "When I went to my office." He fumbled a piece of paper from his pocket and handed it over.

Gannon had never seen Laura Kirby's writing, but somehow he knew at a glance this neat and graceful script was hers before he looked at the signature. He read the brief note in growing alarm:

> Dear Dr. Howard:
>   I couldn't go this morning without at least leaving a word of explanation and apology for deserting you without any warning. It has been a sudden decision, one I know is for the best. I'm returning to Sacramento, and since I won't be seeing you again in all likelihood, I want to thank you for all your kindness and understanding.
>   I'm sorry that Madge didn't feel up to saying good-bye, even in a note. Nobody can be held to blame, but perhaps someday you may understand how badly she has been hurt and disappointed.
>
>   Laura

"They're gone, Frank!" Dr. Howard said hollowly, as Gannon sat staring at the note in a swirl of jumbled emotions. "It's why I went to the stage office—to find out for certain. Both their names are on the passenger list." He hesitated and then asked a question he had been brooding over. "What can she have meant, about Madge being disappointed and hurt and that I might understand someday? Have *I* done something to hurt her? My God! It's the last thing in the world I'd ever have wanted."

Gannon lifted his head and gave his friend a searching look. "You know, of course, the woman's in love with you," he said quietly.

George Howard stared. "*Madge?* Love? I don't know anything of the sort!"

"Then you're the only person around here who doesn't."

The older man stammered in his hasty denial. "Why, the whole idea's ridiculous! She likes me, of course. After all, I tried to make myself useful and help out in any way I could while her husband was dying, and since. I suppose she's bound to feel a certain amount of gratitude, but—it couldn't be any more than that!"

"Are you in love with her?" Gannon asked softly.

Color flooded into Dr. Howard's cheeks at the blunt question. "What's that got to do with anything?" he exclaimed. "Look at me. Why, I'm an old man! If she felt anything, it'd have to be like what she would toward her own father."

"You're sure of that, are you? It didn't occur to you that she might have sense enough not to let a few years make any difference? Because Madge loves you, all right," Gannon assured his friend flatly. "It's no wonder if she's disappointed. You've never given her so much as a hint of encouragement. And now you've gone and let her walk out of your life. Give those boots a kick over this way, will you?" he added, abruptly changing the subject.

Staring at Gannon behind his rimless glasses and moving almost as though unaware of what he was doing, Dr. Howard leaned over and picked up the boots, tossing them toward the bed. But when Gannon started to draw one on, his friend shook his head. "I never said you could go anywhere!" he exclaimed. "Not in the shape you're in!"

Gannon just stared at the doctor. "I don't take orders from you," he said gruffly. "Never mind the shape I'm in. I've got a bad feeling about that stagecoach, and I'm certainly not going to lie here stewing about the danger it could be heading into. Not with Laura and Madge aboard." Ignoring his friend, Gannon shoved his feet into his boots and stood up.

Chapter 13

Before the stagecoach had left Carson City, Laura and Madge had been in their places for some time. When Sheriff Fox and his prisoner boarded the coach, it startled Laura, who had heard nothing of Kramer's arrest. Kramer dropped heavily into his seat, and his face remained expressionless when he noticed Laura. Linus Fox gave her a nod and touched a finger to his hat brim when Laura introduced Madge, who was sitting beside her.

Laura looked again at Kramer. It seemed important to get a response from him, even in the black despair he must be feeling over his capture and at the fate which lay before him. "How are the burns?" she finally asked.

The outlaw shrugged and showed her his hands, which had been shackled to Sheriff Fox. "They're all right," he grunted. Laura saw they had been rebandaged and looked at the sheriff, who said, "That doctor you work for—Howard—I had him come to the jail last night for a look at my prisoner. He said you did a good job, and he put on clean bandages."

Laura nodded. She saw no need to explain that she was no longer working for Dr. Howard or that she was leaving Carson City for good.

The horses were in place and restless to start. The driver—Chuck Drury, who had relieved the wounded Barney Powers—climbed to his seat on the box. Suddenly Laura caught sight of a man who stood off by himself, watching the departure with an air of careful interest.

There was something familiar about the way he stood and about the darkly bearded face that she could not make out too clearly beneath the pulled-down hat. Laura knew she must have seen him before. As though becoming aware of her interest, the man heeled about and quickly walked out of her sight, but not before she remembered one of the men at the shack in the hills—the one named Morg Teale. Still, she told herself, there must be a thousand men with the same unshaven, rawboned appearance in a frontier region like this.

Her thoughts were interrupted when Linus Fox leaned out the window and yelled up to the driver, "Hey! Don't go yet! You've got another passenger." An untidy young man with an untrimmed red mustache came running from the station, one hand holding a carpetbag and the other, which held his ticket, keeping a bowler hat in place. "You traveling with us, Mark?" the sheriff asked out the window. "You almost didn't make it." To the other passengers he added, "This is Mark Twain—or Sam Clemens, whichever he prefers."

Peering inside, the newcomer gave Laura an appreciative glance and also saw that every seat in the coach was occupied. "I guess you're full up," he said. "I'll ride on the box, if the driver thinks he can stand me."

"Hell, I ain't particular. Just hurry it up," answered Chuck Drury.

"Right!" The young man tossed up his carpetbag and then paused for a look at Bart Kramer and the shackles anchoring him to Fox's left wrist. "Would this be the prisoner you came for, all the way from California?" he asked the sheriff. "But I heard he got away from you."

"I got him back," the sheriff said. "Thanks mostly to your friend Frank Gannon. Unfortunately Gannon got himself shot up some in the process. I just hope he pulls through."

Suddenly Laura thought her heart had stopped

beating. She almost cried out as she fumbled for the latch of the door. But she was too late. Clemens had hurriedly scrambled up to a place beside Chuck Drury. A whip cracked, four sets of hooves dug in, and the heavy Concord rocked as the teams leaped into their collars, starting down Carson Street at a dead run.

Sick at heart, Laura dropped back into the seat and felt Madge's hand squeeze her own in a gesture of consolation. As the teams settled into a steady, mile-eating gait, Madge Devere asked Sheriff Fox the question Laura could not bring herself to put into words. "What were you saying about Frank Gannon? Just how badly is he hurt? He's a personal friend," she pointed out.

"Oh! Then I'm sorry. I—I didn't mean to upset anybody," the lawman answered quickly. "He took a bad graze alongside the skull that knocked him out and could possibly have killed him. But it wasn't as bad as it sounds. Doc Howard told me, last night, his pulse was steady and his breathing was good. He gave him every chance of pulling through."

"You're absolutely sure that's what he said?" Madge asked.

"His very words," Sheriff Fox insisted. "I wouldn't lie to you, ma'am. Believe me."

Madge and Laura exchanged looks. "That was last night," Madge pointed out. "Did you hear anything more or see either of them—anything this morning?"

The sheriff shook his head. "I wish there'd been time. But I had my prisoner to collect and a stage to catch."

"I see. Of course . . ." Madge's voice faded away, disappointed.

There seemed nothing more to say, and a moody silence fell inside the stagecoach. Ironically, the morning promised a fine spring day. The rains that had spoiled much of the week were gone, and the world sparkled in sunlight. They rolled on to the steady rhythm of horses' hoofs and turning wheels, the sway of the coach on its broad leather straps lulling the passengers pleasantly.

Laura stared at her hands, knotted tensely together in her lap. Suddenly she turned to her companion. "I have to go back! I *can't* leave him now, Madge. I'll get off at Genoa and wait there for the return coach," she said in a small voice.

Her friend started in alarm. "Now you wait!" she exclaimed, keeping her voice low. "I know how you feel, but you don't want to make a mistake! Suppose you go hurrying back and find that he's all right. What's he going to think? That you're deliberately throwing yourself at him?"

Laura hesitated, but then shook her head. "It doesn't matter. There's at least a chance I could be of help."

"But not unless you're *asked!*" Madge insisted. "Surely you can see the difference. Here's what you do," she suggested. "Send a telegram from Placerville. That will give George time to have learned something definite. Ask him for particulars, and offer your services and training in case they're needed. I'm very sure you'll find out everything is going well. But if George should feel that Frank could use your help, *then* you can go back—knowing you'll be appreciated. Now, is there anything wrong with that?"

Laura was silent for a long moment as she considered the plan. At last she nodded and said tiredly, "You're right. Very well, I'll do what you say."

When they made a brief stop at Genoa for a change of horses, Laura asked at the station about Barney Powers and was told the wounded driver was mending nicely. The local doctor had approved Laura's treatment of the wound and had Barney taking it easy in his hotel room until he was well enough to go back to work. Laura would have liked to see him, but there was no time. She left her best wishes for a quick recovery, and the stage rolled ahead with new teams eager to get under way.

The two other passengers—a Salt Lake businessman and a mining engineer from Virginia City, both on their way to California—kept up a desultory conversation; otherwise, the people in the coach rode in silence. Laura was too concerned about Frank Gannon to feel like talking, and Madge respected her mood. Bart Kramer sat like a lump, sunk deep in whatever thoughts worked behind his stolid features. The sheriff seemed ill at ease. He spent much of his time studying the rocky curtain of hills above the road, as though expecting at any moment to see trouble descend in some form and wrest his prisoner from him.

But as the morning passed nothing unusual happened. At noon they rolled into the station at the foot of the Kingsbury Grade, where the tollroad through the Sierras began its abrupt climb west. As they stepped down from the stage for a hurried dinner, Linus Fox asked one of the station tenders, "Have you noticed any unusual activity on the road? Anybody hanging around who acted like they didn't want to be seen?"

The man gave him a close look that did not miss the handcuffs. He shook his head. "If you think somebody has an eye on your prisoner, there's been no sign of them here."

Bart Kramer's expressionless face gave no indication he even heard the exchange, much less that it had anything to do with him.

After forty minutes for the meal, the coach was hitched to fresh teams, and they began the more arduous part of the journey, leaving the valley behind as they started up the mountains, with California lying beyond.

Reb Jackman had rounded up the rest of his gang for the assault on the stagecoach. He, Morg Teale, and two of his other men held back, keeping out of sight behind a slant of granite rock, while Cad Doolin and another man rode to the relay station. It was set back from the toll road, on a barren flat studded with boulders and brush and a few dwarf pines. The main building and a utility barn were constructed of rock and timber, and there was also a corral containing several of the Overland's sturdy stage horses. A spring brought a steady supply of water. The gang's horses smelled the water, and it made them restless, moving about and causing their riders to swear.

"Here they come!" Morg Teale called.

Four men emerged from the low doorway of the station, two of them carrying guns and the other two with their hands above their heads. Satisfied, Jackman led the way out of the rocks and down to the group before the station.

"No trouble at all," Doolin reported as the other gang members dismounted. "Seein' only two of us, they never suspected nothin' until it was too late. Minute we pulled our guns, they give up without a fuss."

One of the station hands demanded belligerently of Jackman, "What's this all about? What do you figure to do with us?"

His only answer was a cold stare. "Bring them along," Jackman told his men. "We have to get them out of sight. We'll put them in the barn along with all but a couple of our horses." Reins were quickly gathered up, and herding the prisoners, Jackman's gang walked back to the barn.

It was constructed crudely but solidly, with stalls, bins of grain, racks of equipment, a blacksmith's forge, and tools for making emergency repairs to the big Concords. After a quick inspection, Jackman ordered the horses put into the stalls and some feed tossed down for them, but with their saddles left in place. He pointed to the station hands. "Tie them up and gag them," he said.

"No!" The noisy prisoner started to struggle free but one of the outlaws clipped him with a gun barrel. He dropped senseless to the dirt floor. Seeing that, his companion turned white and submitted without a struggle. Jackman left two of his crew to tie both prisoners and returned to the station with Morg Teale and the rest.

Suddenly Teale shouted a warning—a rider in a flop-brimmed hat and corduroy coat was leading a packhorse. He had come from the west, and seeing the relay station he had turned off the road and was approaching the buildings at a leisurely pace. "Take cover!" Jackman told the others. "You won't need that," he added sharply as Teale started to draw a gun. "I'll handle this."

The others dropped from sight behind the building but watched closely as their chief stepped out to meet the horseman a distance from the station. Jackman tilted back his head as the other man spoke to him from the saddle. They talked for a minute or two, but their voices were an indistinct murmur to the watching outlaws. Then Jackman nodded and stepped back. The horseman touched a finger to his hat brim, pulled rein, and started for the toll road. Jackman watched him go for several minutes before trees and rocks finally swallowed the man and his horses.

Teale and the others came out to meet Jackman as he returned. "It wasn't anything," he told them. "He wanted to know something about distances and I told him. He took me for the station agent."

But Morg Teale scowled. "I don't much like this. Too much traffic on this road. What if he'd come by just at the wrong minute?"

"If you'd only been on that stage like I ordered you, any place would have served for us to take it over," Jackman reminded him.

"Wasn't my fault! What were the chances of finding that lady doctor on board? Had she recognized me, one word from her would have put me in a jail cell and likely tipped off the law as to what you were planning to do. I couldn't risk that!" the outlaw insisted.

"Nobody's blaming you," Jackman muttered roughly.

Teale was still not satisfied. "Don't forget that I damned near killed a horse getting you the word in time so you could make other plans," he angrily pointed out.

"Barely in time." Jackman glanced at the angle of the sun, judging the hour with an outdoorsman's eye. "That coach should be along almost any minute." He cast a slow look around at the silent buildings and at his men standing by awaiting their orders. "Something's not right," he said worriedly.

"I dunno what the hell you mean," Teale said, also glancing around.

Jackman's hawkish features had dropped into an uncertain scowl. Suddenly he swore. "That's it!" he exclaimed, turning to his men. "Horses! When they come in they'll be expecting to see fresh teams out and ready for harnessing. Otherwise, the driver is going to know something here's not quite right! Quick! Go fetch them out of the corral!"

Leaving Teale in charge of the horses, Reb Jackman turned to check out the interior of the low-roofed stone station building.

Like most of the Overland's swing stations, its sole function was to supply the big Concord coaches with relays of fresh horses and was large enough to accommodate only the two or three men assigned to it. A couple of bunks, a sheet iron stove, a table and benches, and shelves for supplies were all the crude furnishings. Jackman walked about the room, poking at things. Finding a coffee mill and a sack of beans, he put them on the table and was looking for a pot when Morg Teale's warning shout interrupted him.

Jackman hurried out, nodding impatiently as Teale told him the stage was coming. The nearing rumble of wheels and hoofs was clearly audible. Three of his men were leading the horses from the corral, to serve as bait for luring the unsuspecting coach into the trap. Others of the gang were hurrying from the barn. "Hurry! Get into cover!" Jackman shouted to them. "You all know what you're supposed to do. Stay out of sight until you get the signal."

*   *   *

More exhausted than she had realized by a sleepless night and her anxiety over Frank Gannon, Laura Kirby had finally dozed off. The slowing of the stagecoach roused her. Only half awake, she heard the merchant from Salt Lake asking, "How long do we stop here?"

"Just to switch teams," Sheriff Fox answered.

Laura lifted her head and glimpsed the low-roofed stage station, which she thought she remembered from her earlier trip.

Good Lord, she thought dully. *Was it only a few days ago?*

How much had happened in that brief time—as though her life had undergone an earthquake, throwing everything askew and pointing in some new direction that she could not yet begin to see. She laid her head back against the seat, dimly aware of activity around the halted stage. She scarcely heard Chuck Drury call testily, "Hurry up! We ain't got all day to get these horses changed. You fellows don't act like you know what you're supposed to be doing."

A shadow fell across the window beside her. She opened her eyes and looked into a face she instantly recognized. It was the gun in his hand and a startled curse from one of the male passengers that jarred her fully awake. "Don't nobody try nothin' like reachin' for a gun!" Cal Doolin warned them.

The coach was surrounded by armed men. The door was suddenly wrenched open and a new face appeared in the opening—hawk-featured, with a straggle of graying whiskers on gaunt jaws. The newcomer waved a heavy revolver and snapped, "Everyone sit easy and you won't be hurt."

All at once Bart Kramer was galvanized out of his lethargy. "Reb!" he exclaimed. "Am I glad to see you! I got your message but I was beginnin' to get a little nervous."

"No need to be," the man assured him. "I keep my word. Now come out of there," he added, with a jerk of the head.

"Can't," Kramer said, and he pulled back his sleeve to reveal the handcuffs linking him to Sheriff Fox's left wrist.

Reb Jackman scowled. Even before hearing his name, Laura had known this man with a fanatic's mad gray eyes must be the leader of the outlaws. She watched him gnaw at the inside of one gaunt cheek as he glowered at Linus Fox. "All right, you," he said harshly. "I want the key."

The lawman returned his look without any sign of fear. "I don't have it."

"Like hell!"

Fox shrugged. "Want to search me?"

"Damn right!" the outlaw exclaimed. "Both of you get out right now! Cad, keep an eye on the rest."

Awkwardly the sheriff and his prisoner climbed from the coach while the other passengers watched tensely. Jackman plucked the gun from Fox's holster, then ordered one of his crew, "Frisk the bastard. I don't care if you hurt him some—*I want that key!*"

Fox submitted to the search, but his cold stare had its effect, because the man used caution going through the lawman's clothing. He searched thoroughly and finished with empty hands and a shake of the head as he looked at his chief. "If you want to know, I left it in Carson City," Linus Fox said. "The only duplicate is in my desk at San Andreas. I lost this prisoner once; I wasn't taking any chances on it happening again."

Jackman peered at the lawman with such rage in his eyes that Laura almost thought he was going to shoot the lawman down right where he stood. But he managed to keep a rein on his emotions. Turning to Doolin he ordered, "Cad, take them out to the barn. I saw some tools there, and an anvil. I want them used to knock those handcuffs off. Get one of the others to help you."

"Sure, Reb," Doolin said, motioning to one of his fellow outlaws. Together they marched the sheriff and Kramer to the barn. Reb Jackman watched them go, scowling.

The decoy replacement teams had been returned to the corral, and the men who had held them joined their leader at the stagecoach. Jackman turned to the people inside, but before he could speak, Morg Teale was suddenly beside him. Teale was furious. He thrust his face close to Jackman's and spoke in an angry whisper meant only for his leader's ears. But Laura was sitting by the open window and she heard every word distinctly. "Reb, what are you doing? We ain't got time to fool with them damned cuffs."

"What do you want me to do?" Jackman retorted.

"Ain't it obvious? Shoot 'em both, and let's get the hell outta here."

"Shoot them? Bart Kramer, too?"

"Why not? After he tried to walk out on us? You already told me you decided it was time to get rid of him."

"Only when I'm ready," Jackman corrected the other man. "Once I've found out exactly what happened in Carson last night and how much talking he might have done. Still, now that you've brought it up—"

He turned and looked toward the open area on the other side of the toll road, where shelving rock and scrub timber piled up to high ground that offered a commanding vantage point. "Since you're the one who's nervous, you just go over there and be our lookout. Any trouble coming, you should see it in time to give us a warning." When Teale hesitated, Jackman said sharply, "That was an order! Get moving."

Teale looked as though he might refuse, but Reb Jackman seemed able to instill a habit of obeying in his crew. Laura saw the moment of rebellion die, and with a shrug and a grimace Morg Teale turned away. He strode directly to a hitching rack where a saddled horse was tied, jerked the reins free, and flung himself astride.

Jackman did not even watch him go, taking obedience for granted. Instead he turned again to the coach. Holding the door open, he waggled the barrel of his gun. "The rest of you people can get out now," he said.

Laura felt her friend stiffen beside her. "Why?" Madge demanded, not budging.

Jackman's mouth tightened dangerously. "Because you're being asked—politely, so far. I want all of you inside the station where it's easier to keep an eye on you. Behave yourselves, and nobody will have any trouble. But you *will* do as you're told!" he added grimly.

Both women hated to leave the protection of the coach, but it was clear they had no choice. Laura drew her skirts about her and, ignoring the hand Reb Jackman offered her, found the metal step to the ground. As Madge joined her, Jackman looked from one to the other before speaking to Laura. "I think you must be this lady doctor I've been hearing about. The one that nearly set my men to killing each other a couple of days ago!"

Laura met his glittering eyes evenly. "Was that my fault?" she asked. "I didn't ask to be there!" She almost forgot her fear of the man as her anger grew. "And I suppose it's not *your* doing that Frank Gannon may be lying dead right now—murdered!"

She thought he would actually strike her, and inwardly she quailed a little at her own boldness. But Jackman merely made a brusque gesture and said harshly, "Go on! Get inside!" They knew better than to try to refuse and began walking toward the station.

The other two male passengers had been ordered out of the vehicle, and Jackman motioned to the pair on the driver's seat, telling one of his men, "Don't forget those two, Brodie."

"I ain't." Brodie already had a gun trained on

them. He waggled a finger and ordered, "Both of you! On the ground."

Sam Clemens and the driver quickly glanced at each other. "After you," Clemens said drily. With a shrug, Chuck Drury stepped with practiced ease to a spoke of the big wheel and from there swung lightly down to the ground. Laura, deep in her own mood of despair, watched Sam Clemens inch across the seat after the driver and then turn to make his own awkward descent. He joined Chuck Drury, who stood as though reluctant to move forward, even when Brodie made a threatening gesture with the gun. "I ain't tellin' you again. Come along!" the guard snapped.

As Laura turned toward the station, she thought she glimpsed a quick flash of brightness, as if sunlight had glanced off polished metal. Puzzled, she paused at the threshold of the building and looked again. And that was how she saw everything that happened.

Brodie had taken his eyes off Clemens and the driver for an instant, and that was long enough. As though it had been a signal, Clemens cried, *"Now!"* and gave Chuck Drury a shove to one side. The driver flung himself to the ground, revealing that he had been helping to mask a shotgun, which Clemens held concealed against his leg.

Laura gasped as she realized the young man must have sneaked the weapon from beneath the seat and somehow managed to bring it with him as he made his awkward climb down to the ground. It must have taken real nerve, she thought as Clemens brought the weapon up to fire.

It might have been clumsiness, or perhaps the shotgun had a hair-trigger action. In any event it went off with a great roar before Clemens had the barrel raised. Its entire load of shot drove into the ground in front of him, where it exploded in a huge, blinding cloud of dirt and debris, while the stage horses snorted in terror. The massive roar echoed between the rock faces cupping the open space. Sam Clemens's shoulders sagged as he realized he was holding an empty shotgun in his hands, evidently expecting to be gunned down where he stood.

Laura's hand went to her throat as she watched Reb Jackman stride over to the redheaded man. There was fury in the set of his shoulders. He savagely grabbed the empty gun out of Sam Clemens's hand.

What he might have done then was interrupted by a sudden shout of panic. "Reb! Look at Brodie! Hell—he's hurt!" one of the outlaws cried.

Though most of the shotgun's charge had gone off harmlessly into the dirt, an edge of its blast—or some ricochet of spent pellets—had caught Brodie. As the dust and smoke lifted they could see him on the ground, twisting and moaning. Both of the man's trouser legs, from ankle to knee, were quickly turning red with seeping blood.

Reb Jackman cursed, but for the moment his rage against the prisoner was forgotten. Instead he ordered Clemens and the stage driver, "The two of you—pick him up and get him inside. Move!" As they shook free of their shock and hastened to obey him, Jackman turned and stared at Laura.

"I guess we'll find out now if you're any kind of a doctor!" he told her. "Get in there and do whatever needs to be done. But this time, I'll be watching to see that you do it right."

Chapter 14

George Howard was not a good horseman, but he refused to let Frank Gannon go out alone in his condition. The doctor stuck to his saddle without complaining about the punishment he took, keeping an anxious eye on his friend and somehow matching the grueling pace that the younger man set. They rode with hardly a pause except to switch their gear to fresh mounts at two of the relay stations along the route. Gannon had to concede that the doctor was making good on his promise not to be a handicap.

There was no time for talking and little to talk about. Gannon was conserving his strength, knowing very well that Dr. Howard thought he should never have gotten out of bed. Actually he felt better than he might have expected. The bright sunlight stabbed at his eyes, and the ache in his head throbbed dully, but it was nothing he could not live with. At first he had been troubled by a hint of double vision, but that soon passed.

Gannon knew from the reports he got at each station they passed that they were gaining on the coach steadily. Estimating their progress, and measuring the movement of the sun across the center of the sky, he was beginning to think at last they could not be far behind the stage. This was confirmed when they met a rider coming from the other direction, a man in a flop-brimmed hat who had a pack animal trailing his horse. They stopped in the road to question him.

"Sure," the traveler said, "I met a stagecoach—couldn't have been more than twenty minutes to a half hour ago. I tried to hail 'em but the driver just whipped up his teams and went by me, like he was leery of having anything to do with strangers."

"On this run they tend to get that way," Gannon told him bleakly.

"I wanted to tell him that I seen somethin' that struck me kind of funny at the station I'd just passed," the man said. "There must have been a half a dozen men hangin' around there when I first sighted the place," he went on in answer to Gannon's questioning look. "But as I rode up they vanished like they'd took cover—all but one, and he walked out and talked to me. Said he was the station agent."

"What did he look like?" Gannon prodded sharply.

"Odd sort of fellow. Gray headed. Pale eyes that sort of bugged out, and big nose."

"Then what happened?" Gannon asked impatiently.

"Nothin', actually," the rider said. "But it made me nervous, thinkin' about those gents that disappeared, and the way the strange guy kept looking me over. I asked a few questions about the road ahead and left. And I was glad to get out of there! Later, when I met the stage, I wanted to warn the driver, but he wouldn't stop to listen."

Gannon thanked the man, and they rode on, but after a couple of minutes he turned to George Howard. "Whoever that fellow talked to, it sure wasn't anybody that works for the Overland. He was talking about Crow Station. It's not far ahead of us. Let's hurry—I'm getting a bad feeling."

The other man nodded. His sweaty face showed his deep concern—concern for Madge that was just as great, Gannon knew, as his own worry over the safety of Laura. After all, Madge was a big reason for the doctor's making the ride in the first place.

They rode in silence as the minutes stretched out. And then the west wind, blowing toward them, brought a sound that made them both draw rein and exchange startled looks.

"I take it you heard that, too," Gannon said.

"Almost like a cannon going off!"

"More likely a large-bore shotgun. The station is just ahead of us," Gannon added. "Something's very wrong! Before I show myself, I want to know what it is."

Motioning Dr. Howard to follow, Gannon pulled off the road toward a jumble of boulders on their left. The ground rose as they threaded their way through the boulders. Gannon went carefully, trying to recall the exact lay of the land. With a sudden word of warning, he halted, and his companion rode up beside him. They looked at the scene before them.

They had emerged in a bay of rock and scrub, where they would blend inconspicuously with the background. From there the ground fell away in an easy slope toward the toll road. Beyond that was the station itself. There was a glint of sunlight flashing on the spring water, the stir of remount horses in the corral, a faint wisp of smoke from the mud chimney of the main building. Otherwise, nothing moved. The familiar shape of one of the Overland's big red Concord coaches stood before the station. One of its doors was open, and the horses waited, droop-headed, in the harness.

Something about it all looked very wrong.

"Madge and Laura are down there?" Dr. Howard asked in the stillness.

"We don't know that anyone is. But we need to find out." Gannon made his decision quickly. "I'm going down. There's good cover most of the distance. The hard part is going to be getting across that road without being seen. But sure as the devil I'm not going to sit and wait for it to get dark!"

"What do you want me to do?" Dr. Howard asked.

"For the moment, nothing. Stay here and keep the horses. We might want them in a hurry. Meanwhile, watch for a signal. And keep your head down," Gannon urged.

"I don't have to tell you to do the same!" Dr. Howard said anxiously as they dismounted. He took the reins of Gannon's mount to hold with his own. Gannon drew his gun and checked the loads, settled his hat more firmly over the bandage, and silently started away.

He measured his progress toward the relay station in cautious inches, moving from boulder to brush clump to scrub timber and managing to stay hidden from any observing eyes inside the buildings below. At last he crouched behind a clump of mountain mahogany as he studied the area before him. He still had to cross the road and the open work area in front of the station.

By bearing to the left, Gannon believed he should be able to cross the road at a point where a boulder interrupted the line of sight from the building. From there, perhaps he could work around and come up on the station from the rear. It was a circuitous route and it would use up valuable time, which was annoying, since he had no way of knowing what might be happening inside the station—or even if anyone was there at all. But he could not see that he had any other choice.

He tensed, ready to make his run, when suddenly a voice called out his name, making him freeze. Slowly he turned his head.

Dr. Howard was coming toward him awkwardly, stumbling with his hands above his head. "Frank!" he repeated, sounding badly shaken.

Behind him, a rider held in one hand the reins of the horses the doctor had been left to guard, while a gun in the other hand was pointed at the stumbling man. Gannon stood motionless, unable to believe the turn of events. The man with the gun called sharply, "If you don't want your friend to take a bullet, you'll throw away that pistol you're holding!"

Gannon weighed his chances and came to the sickening conclusion he had none. Slowly, reluctantly, he straightened from his crouched position and let the weapon fall. He stood waiting as the two men came toward him. Dr. Howard was shaking his head and exclaiming in self-condemnation, "I'm less than no use to you! I never even saw or heard him—I just let him walk up to me and point a gun at my head."

"It was my fault," Gannon corrected him. "I should have realized they'd have a lookout. No telling how long he had us spotted."

"Hell, I seen you right off," the man with the gun assured them. He used the muzzle of his gun to push the hat further back from his face, revealing his balding head.

"You're Gannon, I take it," their captor said. "We've missed our try at you twice, now. It's real accommodating of you to just walk into our hands. I'm Morg Teale. Well—just keep walking. Both of you. With your arms up. I'll be right behind." A gesture of the gun muzzle emphasized the order. The two prisoners raised their arms and started for the station with Morg Teale and their captured horses bringing up the rear.

When they crossed the toll road, the sound of their horses' shod hoofs clopping on the macadamized surface brought the station to life. Three armed men quickly appeared, watching as the unarmed prisoners and the rider in charge of them approached. "What the hell have you got, Morg?" one of the gang demanded.

"A present for Reb," Teale answered. "This one's Frank Gannon, of the Overland stage. The other, judging from the bag I found hooked to his saddlehorn, looks to be some kind of sawbones."

"A doctor? Bring him inside—and his bag, too. Ed Brodie's been shot!" the man said, disappearing inside the station.

Teale dismounted and motioned for Dr. Howard to get the medical bag. The prisoners were ushered inside the station.

Gannon knew the place well, but he was not prepared for what he saw when his eyes adjusted from the glare of the daylight outside. The room was more crowded than he had ever seen it. Several men from the stagecoach had been placed on the floor, out of the way, seated with their backs against the stone wall. He instantly recognized Chuck Drury, the driver, and Sheriff Fox. But he was completely surprised to see Sam Clemens among the others.

Sam appeared to be sunk in private gloom. The sheriff gave the newcomers a bleak look that simmered with frustrated anger. Gannon caught a glimpse of the sawed-off handcuff on the lawman's left wrist and then saw the other half of the cuff circling the wrist of Bart Kramer, who stood across the room with a gun in his hand, guarding the seated prisoners.

With a sudden exclamation, Dr. Howard brushed past Gannon and headed for the end of the room, where a couple of bunks were tiered against the wall. Looking past him, Gannon discovered Madge and Laura. Neither appeared to be harmed. They were standing beside a figure on the lower bunk who lay moaning and twisting. "What's wrong here?" Dr. Howard demanded sharply.

Laura had been looking intently at Frank with an odd expression of mingled gladness and alarm. She stirred herself to answer the doctor's question, running a wrist across her sweating forehead. "A shotgun went off, and part of the charge struck him across the legs," she said in a businesslike voice. "His boots protected him from the worst of it, but one knee has had some damage." The hurt man's trouser leg had been slit to reveal the wound. "I don't know yet how bad it is; this is all anyone's found for me to work with."

She showed the doctor a blunt-bladed clasp knife. He gave it no more than a glance and a shake of his head and then opened his leather bag. "Lucky I brought my probe. We'll find out shortly what's what. I'll need your help—yours, too, Madge." He looked around at the silently watching outlaws. "And some of you better be ready to help hold him down. He's not going to like this."

A new voice spoke sharply. "Gannon!"

With his attention focused on what was happening

at the end of the room, Gannon was slow to respond to the new voice. Morg Teale's hand struck his shoulder, turning and shoving him toward the speaker. For the first time Gannon noticed a man who sat alone at the crude table. The gaunt features and the strange, compelling eyes that peered at him left no doubt in Gannon's mind that he was face to face at last with the notorious Reb Jackman.

The outlaw leader gave a summoning jerk of his head, and Gannon walked over to the table. Jackman was drinking coffee from a tin cup. He had found a plate of cold biscuits and was soaking one of them in his coffee to soften it for his few remaining teeth. "So!" he said loudly. "We meet at last, do we?"

"That's what I was about to say," Gannon answered coldly. "After all the trouble you've been to the Overland, I can't say it's exactly a pleasure to meet this way. Now what have you done with my men?"

"The station crew?" Jackman shoved a dripping biscuit into his mouth and worked at it as he wiped his fingers across the front of his shirt. He swigged the last of the coffee in his cup and set it down. "They're all right—tied up, out in the barn. They can be set loose after we're done. We had to get a little rough with one of them when he tried to give us an argument," the outlaw leader added. "I had nothing personal against him, you understand—or, for that matter, against you or old Ben Holladay."

"No? Maybe you won't take it amiss if we were beginning to think otherwise!"

A cry of agony and a flurry of thrashing from the wounded man on the bunk interrupted them. Dr. Howard straightened abruptly from his work. "Are you going to hold him still or not?" he angrily asked the pair of outlaws who were supposed to be helping him.

Reb Jackman gave the disturbance no more than an irritated glance. Frank looked over to see Laura calmly helping the doctor.

Jackman's attention was now entirely on Frank

Gannon, and with an imperious gesture he waved the
Overland man to the bench across the table from him.
"Sit down!" As Gannon obeyed, the outlaw leader shoved
the tin plate and cup aside and leaned both elbows on
the table. His pale eyes bore into Gannon. He said
suddenly, "I've heard you're from Virginia."

"You heard correctly," Gannon replied.

Jackman's mad eyes glittered. "And just what are
you doing to help the Southern cause?"

Gannon had a sudden premonition that he was in
grave danger, depending on the answer he gave. He
chose it carefully. "Out here, I can't see there's much
anyone could do if he wanted to."

"Wrong!" Jackman straightened and slapped a hand
upon the table. "There's plenty to be done! But it takes
planning and organization and a target. I've found that
out! When the war started I had the notion I could fight
the Yankee element here in the Washoe on their own
terms. I soon learned there were too many of them.
Kill one of the bastards and three more spring up! It
came near to driving me crazy!"

He wagged his grizzled head knowingly. But to
Gannon, the expression in Jackman's eyes was proof the
man was insane.

As Jackman continued, it was hard to say whether
he was seriously trying to persuade his fellow Southerner to join him or if his own fanaticism had finally
carried him past the point of discretion. "What I did
was to drop out of sight for a while. People could think
I'd been killed or left the country if they wanted to. But
I was busy, moving up and down the coast, lining up
men in power who could help me. And when the time
was ripe, I put a crew together—and I struck!"

"You struck at the Overland," Gannon answered
coldly. "What does raiding Holladay's stage line have to
do with helping the cause?"

"It has everything to do with it!" Jackman paused
meaningfully while he eyed Gannon narrowly. In a

different tone he asked suddenly, "Do you know about the Knights of the Golden Circle?"

Gannon kept his face expressionless. "I've heard of them," he said. Who had not? The mysterious brotherhood of Rebel sympathizers permeated every section of the country with its organization and symbols and secret rituals. He demanded bluntly, "Are you saying those are the people you're counting on?"

"They're counting on *me*," Reb Jackman corrected him. "Not to mention the men in this room and the others still at the hideout. The first step was to stockpile the arms we needed—that's where all those silver shipments have been going. Once we have enough guns and ammunition and everything is set—we give the signal."

In his excitement Jackman had begun to drool out of the left side of his mouth. "We cut the telegraph lines and close every road. Break off all communication with the East. In the confusion our people will be able to rise and take over Oregon and California for the Confederacy. At the very least, Abe Lincoln will have to send enough troops to take the pressure off of our gallant armies—and give them the chance to march to Washington and end this war for good!"

As he talked, Jackman's voice had risen and taken on the intensity of his own fanatic vision of success. It rang through the room, and every eye was riveted on him. Even Dr. Howard, Laura, and Madge had left the injured Ed Brodie to watch the exchange between Gannon and the outlaw leader.

Gannon said nothing, but something in his expression caused Jackman to stiffen and his mad gray eyes to narrow. "You don't appear to be convinced."

"Convinced!" Gannon said. "Mister, it doesn't matter how big an organization you've got—it can't be enough to pull off that crazy scheme! Just let one thing go wrong—and something always does—the whole complicated business will crumble and fall apart of its weight."

"You call it a crazy scheme?" Reb Jackman's mouth was tight with anger. "There are some of us with more faith in the cause than you seem to have!"

"Like these?" Gannon threw a glance at the silently listening outlaws. "How many of this crew do you think give a damn about your cause? They're out for their own good. They wouldn't have stayed with you this long except for their share of the loot. You don't believe that, I guess," he went on as Jackman glared at him. "How about it, Teale?" Gannon challenged the outlaw. "Just how much does the fate of the Confederacy matter to you? Or to you, Kramer?"

Bart Kramer knotted his heavy brow in a scowl. "I let Reb worry about that kind of thing. I just do what I'm told."

A voice came from the back of the room. "If I can be allowed to put in word here, that doesn't really make the best sense I ever heard."

It was Sam Clemens who had spoken. As all the attention swung to him, he looked a little abashed at what he had done.

Morg Teale took a menacing step toward the young man. "And who the hell are you?"

"No one in particular," said Clemens, swallowing hard. He obviously wished he had kept his mouth shut, but his stubbornness would not let him back out. He swallowed a second time and plunged ahead. "I'm only the one who heard something that was said by you and this Jackman person less than half an hour ago. They were speaking about you, Kramer," he told the hulking man. "About a plan for killing you! *He* would have done it right then." He nodded toward Morg Teale. "But Jackman said no, they would wait until they got you back to the hideout—or wherever it is they mean to take you from here."

"That's a damn lie!" Teale roared.

Though his face had gone pale beneath his mop of reddish hair, Sam Clemens refuse to yield his ground. "Believe this or not—just as you like, Kramer. But I heard them say you tried to walk out on the gang, and now they no longer consider it safe to trust you."

Kramer's scowl was that of a slow-witted man who had been given too much to think about in too brief a time. His mouth worked slowly as he looked first at his informant and then at Morg Teale, unable to make up his mind what he should think.

Help came from an unexpected source. Laura Kirby's soft voice broke into the scene. "Bart, this man is telling you the truth. I know because I heard it, too—every word that passed between them. Believe me, it was just the way he says it was!"

Chapter 15

Perhaps nobody else could have convinced Kramer. But he had learned to respect and trust Laura, and as he listened to her, belief slowly dawned in his heavy features. His stare swung to Reb Jackman. Consciously or not, the gun in his blistered hand swung also. He said hoarsely, "It's true, then—you only took me away from the law to kill me yourself!" His thick fingers tightened on the trigger.

But it was Morg Teale who fired first. Kramer staggered and was driven back against the rough wall, his face blank and mouth sagging. He dropped to his knees and then fell full length, his arms flung wide, the unfired pistol falling from his fingers. Echoes of the shot, trapped within the walls of the building, stunned everyone as they stared at the dead man. Only as the ringing slowly ceased in their numbed ears, did someone suddenly exclaim, "Listen! I hear a stagecoach!"

There was no mistaking the sound, so thoroughly familiar to everyone in the room—the approaching drum of hoofs and spin of wheels over the macadamized roadway.

All at once Bart Kramer was forgotten. Men turned to the doors and windows, and Reb Jackman was suddenly on his feet. "But this can't be!" he exclaimed. "It's not on my schedule!"

Gannon quickly left his seat. He had spotted the pistol Kramer dropped when he was shot. Almost without thinking Gannon dove from his bench after the gun, wrapping his fingers around it. His move was not unnoticed. He looked up and saw Morg Teale glaring at him above the smoking muzzle of his own gun. Gannon raised Kramer's revolver, and both men fired together.

It seemed impossible any bullet could miss at such a short distance, but Gannon's sudden twisting move saved him from being hit by the bullet fired by Teale. He felt nothing except the jolt of the explosion against his wrist. But Morg Teale's face went slack, and he fell as though something had kicked his legs out from under him.

Gannon did not give the outlaw a second thought. The ear-shattering smash of gunshots and the nearing stagecoach with what looked to be an escort of a half dozen armed and mounted men had thrown everything into confusion inside the station. For a frozen instant the outlaws seemed unable to respond. But Gannon was already lunging to his feet.

Reb Jackman, his gun drawn, was leaning across the table as he tried to peer out through the low doorway. His head jerked around as Gannon approached. Their eyes met. Suddenly Jackman remembered he had a weapon and started to lift it.

But Gannon wanted Jackman for a prisoner and he dived straight at him, across the table. Knocking the gun aside, he slammed bodily into Jackman, sending the rebel leader stumbling backward.

At the same moment the rest of the room came alive once again. The outlaw who was supposed to be guarding the prisoners started to turn back to them, but Sheriff Fox seized the man's legs and brought him down. Instantly Chuck Drury fell on the guard and captured his six-shooter. In the back of the room, where the wounded Brodie was lying on a bunk, Cad Doolin had needed both hands to help hold the injured man quiet. Dr. Howard quickly saw his opportunity. Before Doolin could react, Dr. Howard deftly plucked Doolin's revolver out of its holster.

Gannon had the chief of the outlaws trapped, with a gun rammed against his chest. "Give it up, Jackman!"

he warned harshly. "It's all over! That's Ben Holladay out there, and he's brought the special guards he promised me. Not even you can buck odds like that!"

He thought for a moment the outlaw was going to defy him. Gannon could feel the man trembling against the gun muzzle, and could see the drops of sweat that broke out on his fiercely clenched jaw. It was hard for Reb Jackman to surrender his fanatic dream.

But then, in a single instant, Jackman wilted. The fight went out of him. His features sagged. It was a beaten man who let Gannon take the long-barreled revolver from his unresisting fingers.

Most of Jackman's men followed their leader's surrender. Only one of the outlaws was determined to resist. In the confusion he clubbed his way free with the barrel of a pistol and made it through the door and into the open. He was at the hitch rack, trying to mount a frightened horse as Hank Monk brought Holladay's special coach thundering up. One of the mounted guards around the coach yelled at the fugitive to halt. The man hastily flung a bullet at the guard in answer. Immediately, a pair of guns returned his fire. He was hurled lifeless into the dirt. There was no more shooting after that.

Gannon's first thought was for Laura, but too many other things demanded his immediate attention. He caught a glimpse of her peering at him from across the room, her face white and her expression anxious. He gave her a smile and a wave of the hand to say that all was well. Then he turned away, leaving her to help Dr. Howard with the injured Brodie.

Indicating the bodies of Morg Teale and Bart Kramer, Gannon suggested, "I wonder if somebody could find something to put over them. They're no fun to have to look at." He noticed the stagecoach driver. "Chuck, you'd better get to the barn and see what they did with Jones and Tug Barter—cut them loose and find out if the two of them are all right or maybe need attention."

As Chuck Drury set off at a run, Gannon turned to Reb Jackman. "Come along," he ordered. "You're going to meet the man who's been the chief victim of this crazy scheme of yours. I imagine he'd like to have a look at you."

When Jackman failed to move, Gannon simply clamped a hand on one arm and marched him to the door. The other gang members followed under guard.

Hank Monk had halted his vehicle close beside the other Concord. The door of the special coach had opened and Ben Holladay was just stepping down, with his division supervisor, Merl Lunsford, waiting to follow him. Holladay stared at the prisoner and at the man who lay dead beside the hitching rack. "What's been going on here?" he asked Gannon with no greeting. "It looks like we arrived just in time to be in at the tail end of something! And what in the world happened to *you*?" he added sharply, eyeing the bandage on the side of Gannon's head.

The younger man touched the bandage. "That was last night. Somebody's aim was bad. I'd almost forgotten it. I see you brought the special guards you spoke about. If all goes well we may not be needing them."

Gannon indicated the man beside him. "Ben, this is Reb Jackman—the cause of our trouble. We've got part of his gang here. If we can find out from them where the hideout is, we may be able to round up the rest—perhaps even learn the names of some of the men he's been working for. In any case, I think the backbone of this thing is broken."

Ben Holladay stared at Gannon's prisoner with disbelief. "Jackman?" he repeated. "Do you mind telling me *why*? How has the Overland deserved the treatment you've been giving it?"

The broken man only returned his look with a hint of defiance remaining in his stare.

"I don't think he's talking right now," Gannon commented dryly. "But I already know at least part of the story, and it's quite a yarn. I can fill you in later."

Merl Lunsford, who had been listening to the conversation impatiently, broke in. "And what happens now? Do we take these people to Carson City with us?"

"That's out of the question," Gannon said. "Don't forget we're in California. This is part of El Dorado County. Since they were arrested here, they'll have to go on to the county seat at Placerville."

Sheriff Fox spoke up. "Throw the lot of them aboard the westbound stage, and I'll deliver them for you on my way home. It's good to know that idiot sheriff at Carson City won't be able to get his hands on them or try to hog any of the credit!"

"You're more than welcome to them," Holladay told him. "I'll send a couple of men along to make sure they don't give you any trouble." At a signal from Holladay the special guards took over the prisoners. "How soon can that coach be ready to roll again?" he asked Gannon.

"A matter of minutes," Gannon promised. "I'll see to it."

Chuck Drury returned with the two station tenders, who seemed little the worse for their treatment at the hands of the outlaws. Gannon ordered new teams of horses to be brought out, and the stalled stagecoach was readied to resume its interrupted schedule. For the time being the three dead men, and probably the injured Brodie, would have to be kept at the station.

Gannon turned away, but Holladay called him back. "I'm a man of few words," the Overland boss told him. "I'll just say I'm damn well pleased with what's been done today, Frank. I always like to see proof that I'm right when I pick a man for promotion. I can promise you there'll be some more."

If Holladay expected the younger man to be pleased, he was surprised at the answer he got. "I hope not!" Gannon blurted, almost without thinking. "I appreciate what you're saying, but I'm not sure I could handle a bigger job. I like the one I've got. I like the chance to get into the field and work alongside the rest of the men. If you sit me alone at a desk and pile paperwork in front of me, I'm afraid I'd go crazy. You'll do us both a favor if you leave the big jobs to fellows who have the brains for them—like Merl Lunsford."

Holladay blinked, as though taken aback by a reaction he had never encountered before. But then he wagged his bearded head and chuckled. "If that's really how you feel, then I have to respect it because you probably know best. But don't worry. We'll find you something good, along your own line."

As they were shaking hands, Gannon looked behind Holladay and saw the expression on Merl Lunsford's face. The man seemed to be in a state of shock, but he pulled himself together and put out his own hand. "Good work, Frank," he said gruffly. But for the first time Gannon could remember, there was something like approval—and even friendliness—in the man.

Suddenly it occurred to Gannon that Lunsford's hostility could have been rooted in insecurity, in the fear that Gannon might be a rival and a threat to his own position with the Overland. Perhaps he finally understood that the threat had never existed except in his own mind.

Free at last to attend to matters that he really cared about, Gannon headed for the station building. Outside, he saw Linus Fox and Sam Clemens talking together with Hank Monk, passing around a bottle that Monk had apparently brought with him on Holladay's private coach. Clemens still looked a trifle pale after his ordeal, and Gannon paused long enough to tell his friend, "I'm glad to see you're okay."

"By whose standards?" Clemens demanded, frowning. "I didn't exactly cover myself with glory during all this!"

"Oh, come on!" Gannon protested. "It would take nerve for anyone to speak up to Morg Teale the way you did!"

The redheaded man shrugged the words aside. "Maybe. But you didn't see my performance with that shotgun! There I was, trying to act the hero—and it's a wonder I didn't take my own leg off!" He shook his head, the bushy red mustache bristling. "No, sir! I can tell you now, this is one incident no one's ever going to read about in my autobiography!"

Gannon turned to Linus Fox. "After all your trouble, you're going home without Bart Kramer. Too bad," he said, genuinely sorry for the lawman.

"That's how it goes sometimes." Fox accepted the bottle from Hank Monk and wiped the mouth of it on the heel of his palm. "All we could have done with Kramer was hang him. This saves the county the cost of building a gallows."

As Gannon walked away he heard the sheriff suggest to Clemens, "Say, Mark, if you're on the lookout for story material, you ought to drop by my bailiwick. Calaveras County, that is. You'd hear a yarn or two there that even you can't top."

Near the door of the station, Dr. Howard was just straightening up from laying a blanket over the outlaw who had been cut down in trying to escape. He settled his rimless glasses into place and somberly shook his head. "Three dead—all in a matter of minutes!" he said sadly. "And this is just a hint of what we might have seen, if Jackman and his friends had really been able to bring their war here to our part of the country!"

"How are Madge and Laura taking everything?" Gannon asked anxiously.

"Like troopers! Laura did a real fine job helping me with that fellow Brodie. His legs were pretty badly torn up, and that one knee may never be right. I think he'd better not be moved for a while."

"Holladay wants the rest of the gang put on the westbound stage right now and hauled to jail in Placerville." Gannon hesitated. "I'm wondering what the women are going to think of traveling with them."

"Madge isn't going." The doctor caught Gannon's look of surprise and grinned. "We had a chance to talk.

Turns out you were dead right about her—and me. The upshot of it is, she's coming back to Carson City."

"I'm glad to hear that," Gannon said sincerely.

"Now it's *your* turn to do some persuading." Suddenly remembering something, the doctor reached into his pocket. "Tell me, could this be what I think it is?" He gave Gannon a ring with a bright red stone. It would have been easy to believe it was a genuine ruby. "There's words engraved inside: 'To Jim from Laura.' "

Gannon stared numbly at the ring and at his friend. He knew the answer to his question even before he asked it. "Where did you get this?"

With the jab of a thumb, Dr. Howard indicated the dead man lying at their feet. "He was wearing it."

Inside the station building, all was quiet after the recent turmoil. Madge was trying to make the hurt Brodie more comfortable. As Gannon entered, Laura turned from staring at the tarp someone had spread over the still figure of Bart Kramer. She put out her hand, and her fingers felt cold as they tightened on Gannon's. "It's all over," he assured her.

"I know." She looked down again at the still shape on the floor. With a shake of her head she said impulsively, "Do you know, I can't help feeling very sad about him. He was so at odds with the world. Probably no one in his life ever treated him decently. And it finally came to this." She sighed regretfully. "Even so, perhaps it was better than having to face what he knew would be waiting at the end of the stage journey."

She turned away. Gannon followed, drawing a deep breath for what he hated to have to tell her. "Laura . . ." As she looked at him questioningly, he opened his hand with the ring. "Just now—Doc found this."

Laura stared at the little spot of color on his palm and caught her breath. "On—one of *them*?"

Gannon nodded. "It's too late to ask the man questions. But I suppose this gives you the answer to any questions that you still might have about what really happened at Aurora."

Silently she took the ring. She stood looking at it a long moment, her face turned so he was unable to read whatever might be reflected in it. Finally she shook her head and said in a dull voice, "It's like closing the book on a chapter of my life, one that ended long ago."

If Laura had been looking at him, Gannon did not know if he would have found the courage to say what needed to be said. But it was the only chance he would ever have, and with something like a prayer he groped for the right words. "Doc tells me Madge has changed her mind—about leaving Carson City. I was just wondering . . ." His voice trailed away.

"What?" she asked in an odd voice as he faltered. He drew a breath and plunged ahead.

"Laura, is there any chance of you changing your mind? I have no right even to suggest it. I've got no claim on you. But just the same—damn it, that town is going to be the emptiest place in the world for me now if you aren't there!"

She did look at him then, and as he saw her shining eyes, the words he was struggling with died.

"Please stay," he said, firmly but with tenderness.

Now her eyes were even brighter, this time from her tears. "Why, Frank!" she exclaimed. "You really didn't know how desperately I've been waiting, just to hear you ask that!"

Coming in September 1984 . . .

FROM THE
CREATORS OF WAGONS WEST

STAGECOACH

STATION 14:

CIMARRON

HANK MITCHUM

They struck with a cunning and deadly swiftness. Three
outlaws—one of them a young woman whose babyish face
masked a cold sadistic nature—hell-bent on stealing a
strongbox full of gold hidden in the stage headed for the
Cimarron mining camp. Leaving a corpse-strewn trail,
they rode off with the fortune and a terrified hostage:
Helen Bromfield, a woman now desperately trying to
overcome her hatred and fear in the hope of escaping her
captors. One unlikely man is determined to help her: Clint
Dennison, a man forced by circumstances to rob a bank
himself. With a seasoned sheriff on his trail, it's crazy for
Clint to be trying to save Helen instead of his own hide.
But Clint was a man who had never run away from trouble
before—and wasn't about to start now.

Don't miss STAGECOACH STATION 14: CIMARRON,
on sale September 15, 1984, wherever Bantam Books are
sold.

THE EXCITING NEW FRONTIER SERIES
BY THE CREATORS OF

WAGONS WEST

STAGECOACH
by Hank Mitchum

"The STAGECOACH series is great frontier entertainment.
Hank Mitchum really makes the West come alive in each story."
—Dana Fuller Ross, author of *Wagons West*

Here's a powerful new series of adventures set in the West's
most dramatic towns—filled with the danger, history, and
romance of the bold men and women who conquered the
frontier. There's a new STAGECOACH novel available every
other month and the first eight are on sale now.

☐ STATION 1: DODGE CITY (23954 *$2.50)
☐ STATION 2: LAREDO (24014 *$2.50)
☐ STATION 3: CHEYENNE (24015 *$2.50)
☐ STATION 4: TOMBSTONE (24009 *$2.50)
☐ STATION 5: VIRGINIA CITY (24016 *$2.50)
☐ STATION 6: SANTA FE (23314 *$2.50)
☐ STATION 7: SEATTLE (23428 *$2.50)
☐ STATION 8: FORT YUMA (23593 *$2.50)
☐ STATION 9: SONORA (23723 *$2.50)
☐ STATION 10: ABILENE (23858 *$2.50)
☐ STATION 11: DEADWOOD (23998 *$2.50)
☐ STATION 12: TUCSON (24126 *$2.50)

Prices and availability subject to change without notice.

Buy these books wherever Bantam paperbacks are sold or use this
handy coupon for ordering:

Bantam Books, Inc., Dept. LE6, 414 East Golf Road,
Des Plaines, Ill. 60016

Please send me the books I have checked above. I am
enclosing $_____ (please add $1.25 to cover post-
age and handling). Send check or money order—no cash
or C.O.D.'s please.

Mr/Ms_____

Address _____

City/State_____ Zip _____

LE6—6/84

Please allow four to six weeks for delivery. This offer
expires 12/84.